THE EMERALD PORTAL

THE EMERALD PORTAL

CHRONICLES OF THE UNWANTED PRINCESS™ BOOK THREE

J.L. HENDRICKS

MICHAEL ANDERLE

DISRUPTIVE IMAGINATION

Copyright © 2020 LMBPN Publishing
Cover by Fantasy Book Design
A Michael Anderle Production

LMBPN Publishing
PMB 196, 2540 South Maryland Pkwy
Las Vegas, NV 89109

First US edition, September 2020
eBook ISBN: 978-1-64971-180-9
Print ISBN: 978-1-64971-181-6

THE CHRONICLES OF THE FAE
PRINCESS TEAM

Thanks to our Beta Readers:

Crystal Wren, Nicole Emens, Micky Cocker, Mary Morris, John Ashmore, Kelly O'Donnell, Larry Omans, Michael Baumann, Daniel Weigert, Rachel Beckman, Theresa Holmes, Jim Caplan

Thanks to our JIT Team:

Angel LaVey
Dave Hicks
Deb Mader
Debi Sateren
Diane L. Smith
Jackey Hankard-Brodie
Jeff Goode
Kathleen Fettig
Micky Cocker
Misty Roa
Paul Westman
Veronica Stephan-Miller

Editor
SkyHunter Editing Team

DEDICATIONS

Dedicated to all you dreamers out there.
Never stifle your imagination,
and never stop going after your dreams!

— J.L. Hendricks

To Family, Friends and
Those Who Love
To Read.
May We All Enjoy Grace
To Live The Life We Are
Called.

— Michael Anderle

PROLOGUE

The noise inside the protective dome around the slamball field was almost deafening. Every single seat in the stadium was full, and the crowd was crushed together, trying to make room for others to squeeze in. No one should miss this kind of excitement. The World Slamball Championships only came along every four years, and members of the fae community eagerly anticipated the return of this storied event.

The locations hosting the games started preparing for the championships years in advance, often beginning before the last competition was over. They not only needed to make sure the stadium was ready for the players, but also for the fans. Huge crowds swarmed the host cities to attend the games, which meant the people of those cities needed to be prepared for the onslaught.

Hotels and temporary inns designed specifically to cater to the fae, would pop up and start taking reservations. Restaurants increased their seating and expanded their delivery options. Ambitious entrepreneurs designed clothing, signs, and other memorabilia to sell outside the arena.

It was a celebratory, thrilling time, and anyone within the

dome could feel the energy rushing throughout. As freeing as it would be to not have the dome around the field, it simply wasn't an option.

The dome kept the players in line, and ensured fair play, but also concealed them from the humans who may be around. It didn't always work. There were times when wayward humans were drawn in by the spectators coming to the area and would wander into the dome. Since these protective features were designed to blend in with the surroundings and look like something expected in the area, the humans would simply join up with the crowd and walk in. Of course, that was always handled promptly, and the games would continue.

Today, the crowd was hungry for the game, and brimming with excitement to watch the match. Those with the most expensive and exclusive seats sat in their prime positions, peering out over the field. They were content to roam around in their private boxes, chatting with others, and buying refreshments. The rest of the crowd wasn't quite so lucky.

General admission meant getting a good seat was a fight of the fittest. Fans camped out for hours, sometimes a day or two, before the dome opened to allow the spectators in. When the stands opened, it was a mad rush, every fan for themselves, to find a prime spot.

Once there, no one moved. You stayed in your spot and protected it so nobody would come by and steal it. For some, that equated to hours of sitting in the same place, waiting for the game to start.

Now the time had finally arrived, and the anxious energy building in the stands was reaching a fever pitch. The cheering grew louder when the referee walked onto the field. Which was the first sign that the game was about to begin. He held up his hands to settle the crowd, but it took several seconds before the voices died down.

When it was quiet enough for him to speak and actually be

heard, he used a spell to amplify his voice, so it went to every inch of the stadium. He didn't want to take the chance that any of the players or fans would miss what he had to say.

"Hello, fans. And thank you for joining us today. Welcome to the World Slamball Championships!" Another surge of raucous screaming filled the dome, and the referee let it go on for a few seconds before holding his hands up again.

"Before we introduce the teams and get the game started, I want to make the rules very clear. These apply to every single person in attendance today, players and fans alike. Listen closely. Claiming you didn't hear or understand the rules won't get you out of the consequences of not following them, should you make that choice."

Some of the cheering turned to boos, but he wasn't deterred. Presenting the rules at the beginning of the championships was essential. Perhaps more now than ever before. These games were coming at a harder time than any of the championships before, and he knew the risks were higher. It was a reality of the game. Everything was becoming more intense, and it seemed simple things like watching sports had turned into a potentially dangerous event.

"I want a clean game. No funny business. At the start of the game, an additional protective dome will be set up around the playing field itself. This will separate the stands from the players and ensure there is no interference. No magic from the outside of the dome will be able to get inside, and no magic being used within the dome for the game will be able to get outside. I don't want a repeat of what happened four years ago."

He didn't need to explain that any further. Everyone in attendance knew the incident he was referencing.

At the last World Slamball Championships, a particularly intense game had sent magic out into the stands. This, combined with illegal magic being used by a fan who had put down a very high bet on his favorite team and was going to do anything he could to make sure he made good on that bet. The result was devastating, with several spectators suffering serious injuries, and one had died.

The referee didn't want to go into detail about that now. It was important to lay out the rules and make sure everyone followed them, but he didn't want to ruin the fun of the beginning of the Championships by bringing down the energy and excitement.

He elevated his voice over the growing protests. "There will be no intentional harming of any of the players. This includes use of physical force as well as magic."

The booing grew louder, and some of the fans started hurling insults and derogatory slurs at the official.

"No throwing of curses of any kind. No mind-altering spells. Keep in mind there are referees and other officials positioned throughout the area of play as well as in the crowd. Some are in uniform, while others are not. They will be watching everyone carefully, and using spell detection techniques to identify anyone using forbidden magic during the course of the game."

The referee paused and looked around the stadium. Every single spectator felt chills down their spines, as though the ref was singling them out. "Any player caught using any form of prohibited spell or magic will be immediately ejected from the game, and will be considered for permanent expulsion from the games. Teams will not be permitted to call in further players or replace the ejected player with a player not already on their active roster."

"Any spectator caught using any form of prohibited magic on another spectator, player, or official will be removed from the game, all admission forfeited, and their rights to attend any future Games revoked." The referee's hand sliced through the air to punctuate his statement.

The insults became coarser, and the names more egregious. Someone threw an empty cup at him, starting a cascade of trash and balled-up programs tumbling down on him. A swipe of his hand created a barrier around him that prevented any of the debris from hitting him, and a young fae acting as the water boy for the players scrambled to start collecting everything that was thrown.

"Listen carefully," the head referee instructed. "If anyone is found to have used a death curse of any kind on any person within this stadium, they will find themselves being immediately tossed into the Dungeons of Forasaon. There will be no trial and no appeals. It will be up to the head jailer to determine the length of the sentence. His full discretion will be honored without question, and no relief of any kind will be offered. Let this be fully understood. There will be *no* exceptions. For anyone or any reason."

Loud laughter belted out from the crowd in several spots around the stadium, and spectators called to him.

"That may be the only way a halfling gets into Faerie!"

CHAPTER ONE

The edges of the leaves were starting to change as the end of summer wound down on campus at the academy. The sun was still hot and dry and left Mia with little choice other than short sleeves as she strolled to the practice grounds.

She wished the weather would turn crisper, more fall-like, but only three weeks into her senior year, she knew that was a month or more away. Still, a jacket hung by her door, waiting for the first day that cool air would necessitate long sleeves and pumpkin-spiced coffee.

Mia flipped to a familiar song on her phone and lost herself in her thoughts and the music as she went down the path leading to the practice grounds behind the academy. Students were milling about, some finding sunny places to sit and study, others playing various forms of outside games, but nearly all of them wearing an insignia on their shirt or hat.

The logo of the Academy Slamball team shone from their gleaming gold pins. The World Championships were coming soon, and that meant more portals, more excitement, and more opportunities to lose herself in a shared experience, and not have the heavy thoughts of the summer weighing on her.

"Not doing this today," she muttered, calling out her brain for wanting to dive back into the mopey, homesick, and guilty part of her consciousness.

Spending a few weeks with her father had been wonderful, but not nearly long enough, though at the same time, it had seemed ages away from her friends and her new life. A new life her father still knew nothing about.

She had told him names of friends in passing and rewrote scenarios that happened on campus to fit the narrative, but her father still believed she was studying Wushu in China. He imagined her participating in tournaments, and learning more about the martial art she had dedicated so much of her life to before arriving at the academy.

Thankfully, she and Luna had spent time each week working on martial-arts training during her second semester at the academy. This year, Mia had plans to spend more time honing her skills and ensuring that she continued to learn more and more about her chosen art form.

Mia hated lying to her father, but it was essential, both to protect him and to protect herself. To make sure that no one in her outside world knew where she was. Even Becky didn't know the truth. And she shouldn't, she couldn't.

Returning to campus had been a difficult transition since part of her longed to be with her father. But still, she enjoyed learning about her powers, honing them, and spending time with her new set of friends. Even Vivi... Mostly.

Lost in her thoughts, Mia nearly missed the small dirt path leading into the heavily wooded area surrounding the practice fields. A solid, slightly shimmery dome rose in the middle, a sign of the group's increasing power and control. Now each of the five could hold the protection in place on their own without thinking about it. Their individual shields had a faint color tint and, if you knew what you were looking for, you could tell who was casting it. Today's had the slightest touch of periwinkle blue, and Mia smiled. Luna had the job.

"Mia, you made it," Carson called from across the field.

A floating purple orb hung in the center of the group's circle. Mia recognized it as a bender, a type of physical object that magic can manifest. When used correctly, it can literally bend reality, at least temporarily. Useful in fights with large groups, the bender can convince entire armies that not only are they naked and without their armor, but that their enemies are giant spider-creatures, or whatever else the casters decided to concentrate on. As usual, it wasn't something students of Mia's age ever did, but Zander was determined that perfecting this spell would be the key to acing their final scores.

"Sorry, guys, I thought you might want to see this." Mia held out the pamphlets that had been slipped under her door. Curious, the rest of the group allowed the bender to dissipate, and when it was well and gone, they crowded around her, each taking a copy.

"They're setting up new portals to get to Scotland for the Slamball Championships," Zander read.

"We don't need permission to go see other games," Carson noted.

"As long as we don't miss any classes." Vivi moaned. "How do they expect us to enjoy the tournament if we have to make sure we hit all our classes?"

"You just want to see the Highland team, don't you?" Carson teased. His voice held a trace of jealousy that Mia almost didn't pick up on.

"Angus McIntyre is a gift from the gods, and deserves to have his loyal and loving fans by his side," Vivi responded, deadpan. Mia tried to choke back a laugh, but the sound was audible enough that Vivi shot her a glare. "Like you don't want to see those vampire boys from Germany?" she teased.

"I have *one* poster, and it came free in a box of candy." Mia was trying not to laugh harder, or let on that Vivi might be right.

"We can take turns going to some of the non-school games, and take notes for each other," Zander interrupted, taking their attention off their petty bickering. "Vivi, you and Carson can go see the Highland teams, and I'll go with Mia to see the German team. I've been meaning to scout their forwards for a while, anyway."

"I'll tag along with Luna," a voice from behind Mia said, and she turned to see the small speck of a creature flying over her shoulder toward Luna. Cinder circled Luna a few times, and settled at eye-level, joining the group as though she were another student.

"Maybe we can see the Highland Games, as well?" Luna waggled her brows at Vivi, who didn't pay any attention to her.

Cinder laughed and nodded.

"You want to go with her?" Vivi said to Zander, and it was her turn to reveal a touch of jealousy in her voice.

Zander appeared to ignore her and walked to Mia. "Let's take a break for a while, guys. Good job today. I'll see you all at six," he said, referring to when their evening Human History class would start. Mia moved toward Luna, intending to ask if she wanted to walk with her back onto the campus grounds, but Zander interrupted. "Hey, Mia," he said.

"Yes?" Mia asked.

"Want to walk back with me? Since we have the same next class and all." Zander was referring to their Applied Mathematics class.

"Sure," she said, fighting the feeling that someone had turned the heat up from its already uncomfortable oppressiveness. She grabbed the bottled water from her bag and took a massive swig, hoping he didn't see the flushing of her cheeks.

Zander fell into step beside Mia as she walked toward the campus. In the distance, a few teachers were opening yet another portal on the grounds, this one closer to the athletic department buildings, and most likely for the exclusive use of their own

Slamball teams. Mia watched them with interest for a few moments before Zander spoke.

"I feel like we haven't really talked much since you got back. How was your break?" he asked.

Mia paused before responding. Distilling all the emotions and deception, along with the comfortable and relaxing boredom of being at home with her father, plus considering the few weeks spent shadowing Cassia on her assignments and hunting for Narco, was a challenge. She exhaled slowly.

"It was good." For a moment, she thought about leaving it at that. An uninspiring and inadequate response.

"Just good?" Zander's hopeful expression turned to disappointment, as though he had hoped for more from her.

Mia couldn't just let him down, especially since it wasn't the whole truth. "Well, it was crazy, actually. I went home to see my dad and stayed there for a few weeks. It was like I never left. I was a little kid again, you know? Regular bedtime and family dinners at the table and all that. It was like none of this was real for a little while. I liked it, as a break, but after a while, I just wanted to come back. As much as I miss my Dad, I missed being here, learning my power, and all that too."

Zander nodded and fished a piece of gum from his pocket. He offered it to Mia, who shook her head, and he popped it into his mouth.

"What about Narco? Did Cassia find anything out?" he asked.

"No, not really. I actually went with her a couple of times. She thought it would be good for me to get used to the portal system, and hang out with her for a little while, so I went. It's like he disappeared off the face of the planet."

"Maybe he's dead," Zander said. When she didn't respond, he shrugged. "Hey, a guy can hope, right?"

"Cassia seems to think he's in Faerie, living like a hero."

Zander nodded and decided to move away from the

depressing discussion and on to something different. "So, the German team?" A wry smile crossed his lips.

"No, not really. Like I said, it came in a box of candy. I'm still getting the hang of the professional leagues. I'm hoping our academy being in the Senior High competition will help me get to know the teams a bit more. I'm still not sure exactly how all this is working."

"Do you want to know? I don't want to bore you with details," he said, uncharacteristically reserved.

Zander was usually the first to go off on tangents about why things worked and how often, to the rapt attention of Mia and the general boredom of everyone else. Zander prided himself on learning how things worked, including people. Which made him such a strong leader for their group.

Mia nodded.

"Well, it's like the Olympics…in a way. The World Championships is only every four years, so it's a big deal when it happens. In order to get in, you have to be either first or second place in your league from the year before, and the eighteen teams in the tournament are from all over the world. This year, the first round will all take place in the Highlands of Scotland."

"Have you ever been there?" Mia asked.

"Only once, on a school trip. Apparently, they leveled out a bunch of land for the games. Scotland is full of history for fae, but it can be dangerous. Redcaps have a union house in Glasgow, and boggarts are all over the place, so security is usually tight for students. Even more so for the games. That's why Elmhurst is opening direct portals; she doesn't want people wandering off."

It made sense to Mia, especially since the history of the Isle of Raasay was of such importance to both the Seelie and Unseelie cCourts. The area was contested by both Courts and was the subject of various vicious battles throughout history. The patricide which had split the kingdom—creating the two Courts—still reverberated among fae today, even at the academy. Even among their group. She could only imagine that the area surrounding a place of such importance was bound to be rife with chaotic and unpredictable magic, and those who would want to harness it for their own purposes.

"Mia?" Zander asked.

It dawned on her that she had missed something. "Hmm?"

"I asked if you wanted to go to the German team's opening-round game. It's during a period when we don't have classes, and I'd love to check the game out with you."

The addendum of "with you" was not lost on Mia. "Sure, that sounds great." She was attempting to play it cool but was feeling miserable about it.

"Awesome. I'll meet you by the library around eight tomorrow morning, okay? And we'll see about getting tickets to the game."

"Eight then," Mia repeated, and Zander nodded.

It wasn't a date. Not really, anyway. But it also wasn't the first time Zander had specifically asked her to spend time with him. Just the two of them. He told her he wanted to get to know her better, and she knew she wanted the same. It was hard to do much in the way of getting to know each other with their three friends around, so she always looked forward to the bits of time they had alone together.

CHAPTER TWO

Over the summer, Mia had become pretty good at going through portals, but that didn't stop a small, split-second of a stomach flip every time she went near one.

The memory of being so discombobulated last year was very present in her mind, even after going through dozens of portals with Cassia as she shadowed her. By now, it was old hat, and she shouldn't even blink at them, but there was always the slightest hitch of breath every time she stepped close to one before going through. And each time, there was that moment like when a rollercoaster has crested the first big hill, and though you know you are safe, everything in you screams to be let off the ride. That included going to see the games with her group.

"Do you know where this portal goes?" Mia said quietly to Luna as they stood in line. She figured if she didn't use her full voice, the hint of fear wouldn't be present.

"Scotland," Luna responded flatly.

"No, I know that. But where exactly? I know some of them drop off right outside the field, and others are farther out near the cities."

"Some are *in* the cities, actually." Luna turned to look at her.

"As seniors, we are allowed to go to one or two of them, but the teachers are the only ones allowed to go to the others."

"Why only teachers?"

"Bars."

"Oh."

"This one lets us off on the Isle of Raasay." Luna appeared frustrated by the dreadfully slow pace of the line ahead of them.

Various security teams and professors were posted at each portal, checking with the students and making sure no weapons were leaving the school grounds. While that made sense, Mia was nervous about it. She always had her sai on her person, and not having them, heavy and cold, sitting in their holster on her back, was difficult for her to handle.

"We are going to meet Zander, Carson, and Vivi there," Luna added.

Since the other three had a different class than Mia and Luna, they had left for the portal earlier. Principal Elmhurst had moved the class schedule around for that one day so that they all had the afternoon off to go and watch their team's opening game.

"So, have you ever been there?" Mia asked as they took a small step forward. One of the students seemed to be in trouble for something in their backpack, and the audible groan from the line meant more waiting.

"A few times, actually. My grandfather owns part of a brewery in the Highlands. I hope I'll get a chance to see him while we're there. I've never been to any of the big cities, though. Too dangerous for fae to be out there with all the redcaps hanging around. At least in the Highlands, it's only boggarts and wood nymphs. And brownies, but they don't tend to bother anyone."

"Speaking of brownies, where's Cinder?" Mia asked.

"She went ahead with the rest of the group. As a faerie, she's allowed to go wherever she wants without anyone around and is pretty excited to go to the Isle of Skye."

"What's the Isle of Skye?" Mia asked, confused. She had heard a fair amount about the Isle of Raasay in the last few days, but this was new.

"It's where the faeries live. It's supposed to be gorgeous there, but no fae is allowed without an express invitation from the Faerie. Trust me, you do not want a faerie mad at you. But since the games are being held across the water from them, they have extended a blanket invitation to halfling students to come visit, provided they have someone escorting them. The only way a full fae is allowed at all is to escort the students, so there's been a lot of back and forth among the instructors as to who gets to do it. I know Elmhurst will be one of them."

"When you say faerie, do you mean pixies like Cinder? Or a different type of faerie?" The designations still confused Mia. They were all fae, but the word *faerie* seemed interchangeable at times.

Luna frowned and paused. "Yes, I can see how that would be confusing. A faerie is an adjective at times and used to describe most of the smaller creatures who are part of the larger fae group. But these faeries are cousins to pixies. Sometimes, they are even lumped into the same group. And, oddly enough, they look a lot alike."

Mia blinked a few times and processed what she just heard. "I don't think I'll ever get used to the fae and all of their weird names or designations. Why can't we all just be fae? Why do we have to have so many races?"

"Humph. I agree." Luna had always believed there was too much discrimination amongst the fae, but who was she to change up centuries of how they classified themselves?

"When I talked to Cassia, she said she would be attending some of the games. Maybe she could escort us?" Mia asked, not really trying to change the subject, but doing so anyway. Without her weapons, having Cassia around would cut down on a ton of the anxiety Mia was already feeling. Not that she didn't have a trick up her sleeve anyway, but it would still make her feel better.

"I don't think so. The faeries are pretty specific about this sort of thing. It's pretty rare they let anyone on their island at all, so I don't think Elmhurst or anyone else would risk it by letting Cassia in there," Luna said.

Mia frowned. "Looks like the line is finally moving," Mia said, her attention returning to the portal.

Students were now streaming through a bit faster, and Mia soon understood why. A second instructor, one she barely recognized from among the many faces she saw in the halls of the academy, had joined to check students through. In a matter of moments, Luna and Mia stood side-by-side, awaiting the go-ahead.

"No weapons or contraband of any type?" the male instructor asked, opening her bag and doing a cursory glance.

"No, I left the rocket launcher at home." Mia smiled wide. The instructor, who she now remembered was a law professor, did not seem pleased. He stood, stony-faced, looking at her in increasingly uncomfortable silence. Behind her, Mia heard Luna finish up and jump through the portal. "No, no weapons or contraband," Mia finally said.

"Go ahead," the humorless instructor said, and Mia snatched her bag and turned to the portal. A mild butterfly feeling ran through her stomach, and before she could let herself think about it any further, she jumped into the portal.

The best piece of advice Mia had received about portals was to close her eyes. It seemed simple enough, but something about the portals gave her a strange impulse to keep her eyes wide open, as though she might encounter an enemy in the vortex, and needed to see them to fight.

But in the split second it took to go from the grounds of the academy, just outside the cafeteria building, to the soft, cool grass of the Isle of Raasay, there were no enemies. No monsters. Only a blur of time and space and magic, like looking out from the inside of a blender. The sensation of moving very fast—like one of those roller coasters that went from stationary to a hundred miles an hour in seconds—then stopped, and she wavered on her feet for a moment before opening her eyes.

"Move out of the way," came an annoyed voice from behind her, and she realized she had been standing in front of the portal long enough for someone to come behind her and almost knock her over.

Mia spun around, muttering an apology, and stepped away. The Isle of Raasay was gorgeous, just like Luna had said. A lush green field of grass was broken in the middle by a gray winding road, weaving and turning toward the horizon.

On one side, the water sparkled in the sun, and when the light hit it at exactly the right angle, it looked like a sea of emeralds. Above it, wispy white clouds floated by in an endless blue sky, and the air was crisp, just the way Mia had wished for on campus. It was enough to make her pull her thin jacket around her tighter, and remind herself that next time, she needed something heavier.

Craggy rock formations grew from the ground at random, some rising many stories high, and formed shapes that resembled giants against the setting sun. There was magic here, not in the traditional sense of spells and curses, but the enchantment of the surroundings, which relaxed her, and piqued her interest in exploring it all at once.

"Mia, over here," Zander shouted from a few dozen yards away. Luna was nearly a third of the way there and turned to Mia, seemingly confused. She doubled back a few steps, and Mia met her halfway.

"I thought you were right behind me," Luna said, a slightly embarrassed smile on her face.

"Apparently." Mia smirked.

"Well, I was walking along, talking to nothing," Luna said, laughing. "Come on, the rest of the group is waiting for us."

As they reached the crew, Mia noticed Carson was decked out

in full academy gear. His pants were school colors, and his sweater had ELMHURST emblazoned on the front, a pin just above the heart, and a big hat with ELMHURST across it as well. Of course, that was subdued compared to the neon, glowing and blinking fake glasses he was wearing.

"You look, uh…festive," Mia said.

"And you look boring," Carson responded. "It's called team spirit, Mia."

"It's called spending an hour in line because they have to check all those pockets and make sure your glasses aren't a bomb." Vivi pouted. "I wanted to be at the arena thirty minutes ago, but Mr. Showoff here had to put on every stupid thing in his closet."

"Well, it's a good thing, since we got held up as well," Luna said.

Vivi cracked a mirthless half-smile that said she likely would have pouted about that too but would have had no issue—zero—leaving Mia and Luna behind if possible.

"Well, we're all here now," Zander said, "so let's go get our tickets and get to the arena."

"Who has our tickets?" Mia asked.

"Elmhurst." Vivi's tone was gloomier. "It's like the world wants me to be miserable."

"She's just upset because she was hoping to squirrel away with one of those Highland team guys," Carson joked.

Vivi's glare spoke volumes about how realistic that scenario was. "She's going to be on top of us the entire time. I know it. Forget having fun, she'll shush us for cheering too hard," Vivi complained.

"Elmhurst will be fine. She's the one who insisted all the students get to go to our academy's games after all. If she didn't want us to have fun, she wouldn't have made it so easy to come." Zander was ever the voice of reason. Vivi seemed less than convinced.

As they walked toward the arena where the first game was set to begin, Mia took in the surroundings a little more. The peacefulness of the area was intoxicating, the type of peacefulness that didn't seem real. Certainly, the effect of magic was at work here, and she enjoyed the almost electric crackling in the air of so many beings capable of harnessing that elemental power all joining together in a place so full of it. Added to the picturesque view was the clean, crisp air tinged with salt from the sea, and Mia was certain this was the most perfect place she had ever been.

In the distance, the Isle of Skye called out to her, with its similar craggy shoreline and lush, green fields. Only the faerie went there unless expressly invited, Luna had said. Mia wanted to learn more, not just about the land but the people. The infamous story of the patricide that had created the Seelie and Unseelie intrigued her. So lost in her thoughts, Mia barely noticed a figure in the distance, watching her; unmoving, hands clasped behind her back. Until suddenly, recognition filled Mia's face.

It was Cassia. Beside her stood Elmhurst, and they were speaking to each other in low tones. When the group reached them, Cassia took Mia aside. Elmhurst motioned for the others to follow her, and Mia realized she would be playing catch up yet again.

"Hey, I just wanted to check in with you and let you know I was around," Cassia said.

"Thanks. Aren't you coming to the game?" Mia asked. Cassia looked around for a moment, appearing to be thinking about something.

"No, not today at least. I have some other things to take care of. Mia, just listen to me. Be careful out there. Stay with your group. And if you need me, I won't be too far away."

With that, Cassia left, and Mia returned to her friends, too excited to worry what Cassia's warning may have foretold.

CHAPTER THREE

Mia and her compatriots roamed around the dome in awe. The protective dome was erected over the area of the games to shield the events from humans, and to contain all the magic inside it. It was similar to the ones they had created on the academy campus when they had enjoyed the carnival celebration and the snowball fight, but much larger and more elaborate.

Those domes had only needed to shield the field behind the school building, or the field outside town when the Five used them to conceal their practice efforts. This dome was different. It had to contain the massive stadium structure which hosted the Slamball Championships as well as prevent passersby from noticing the major changes to the landscape in order to accommodate the Games.

Regulations regarding the stadiums used for the World Slamball Championships were very precise and had to be followed exactly. Much like the Olympics in the human world, cities vying to host the Games had to put in a bid many years before the championships. In that bid, they had to demonstrate they not only had a location with enough physical space to hold the stadium, but that any modifications necessary to fulfill the regulations could, and would, be made.

When it came to *this* arena, one of the major modifications needed to create the stadium was to level the ground. The natural rolling hills and moors of Scotland were not the right topography to build a Slamball stadium.

Fortunately, spells could perfectly level the ground to make it possible to build the stadium. After the conclusion of the games, The officials would put the land back the way it had been, and no one going past in the days to follow would be any the wiser.

But that did mean anyone familiar with the area would notice the major changes if there wasn't enough of a shielding precaution. Mia was surprised to learn, however, that all humans were not kept in the dark about the Games.

"Those people standing around at the edge of the grounds," she said casually, not wanting to sound confused or like she didn't know what was going on, even though that was exactly the case. "They didn't seem…"

She trailed off, and Zander looked at her with a smile. "Like us?" he offered.

Mia nodded. "Were they human?"

"Yep," Vivi answered, but didn't give any more explanation.

The dark-haired Unseelie reveled in the idea of knowing something Mia didn't. The stronger Mia became, and the more her powers revealed themselves, the more insecure and unsure of herself Vivi felt. She had worked her entire life to build her skills and become as strong as she was. Even with the uncomfortable reality of being forced to work alongside Seelie halflings, it was a tremendous honor to be chosen by Elmhurst.

Being part of the Scooby Gang was validation, confirmation that everything she did was worth it, and that her efforts would one day be rewarded. Then Mia had come along, unaware of who or what she was. She had no training and had instantly become the darling of the school. Even when she messed up, she was still adored and admired.

Gradually, Vivi was growing closer to Mia and didn't have quite the same level of disdain for her that she had when the red-headed halfling first appeared at the school. But that didn't mean she'd made a complete change. It still amused her and gave her a little extra boost when she knew something Mia didn't.

There was always that reminder that Vivi was born into the fae world and had spent her entire life knowing who she was. That gave her the connection to the culture, ways, and traditions which Mia was still trying to learn. This was one of those situations.

Mia stared at her, waiting for something more, but Vivi simply kept walking, pretending to be fully engrossed in the happenings all around them.

"Okay," Mia said after several seconds. "That was helpful. Thank you, Vivi."

Luna walked up beside Mia and shook her head. "Don't mind her. Yes, those are humans. They are the locals of the island who have lived here for generations. They all know what's going on."

"They know about the fae?" Mia asked, shocked.

"They do. Not only do they know about the fae, but they interact with them regularly. All of them come from families who have been serving the fae for many years. In fact, the first humans who ever came to the island were brought onto the island from the mainland, specifically for the purpose of serving the fae. Both sides have cooperated peacefully," Luna told her.

"So, they know about the Games?" Mia asked.

"Yes. That's why they're around. They know how important the championships are to us, and that we don't want to have any human interference. If it became a problem, or there were too many humans who caught wind of what was going on, there could be some very serious consequences. The Games might be discontinued. So, the locals on the island help every time there's a championship here. Their job is to stay near the edges of the grounds and keep the uninformed away. They come up with reasons why the area is being used and is inaccessible, and the humans trust them. They're very beneficial to us."

"And it's fun to do some human watching," Carson said. "You never know what they're going to do when they're around us."

It still struck Mia as strange to hear the other halflings talk about humans as if they were a somewhat foreign concept. Even the ones with close ties to the human sides of their families, or who were raised by their human parents, often talked about them as if they didn't fully understand them. But she supposed that was to be expected. They were raised in the ways of the fae and didn't have the same exposure to a fully human life that she'd had. For those who had spent most of their time with their fae parent, the world of the humans seemed odd.

"Can you believe this place?" Zander steered the conversation away from the humans as if he could tell it was making Mia uncomfortable. "They really went all out for the championships this year."

"It feels like it's been forever since the last one," Carson said.

"He only says that because his favorite team lost the last one, so he's decided to wipe it from his memory," Vivi quipped.

"I still say there were some funny dealings going on in that last game," Carson insisted. "That just didn't make any sense."

"They lost by fourteen points," Luna pointed out.

"Exactly! When does that ever happen?" Carson asked.

"When one team is nowhere near as good as the other," Zander said.

They all laughed and walked through the dome. The area where the games would be played was set up toward the back of the dome, with player dressing rooms and lounges behind it. The rest of the dome was filled with concession stands, merchandise booths, games, and vendors. All set up to appeal to the masses.

Many of the spectators were already crushed into their seats in the stands.

Their general admission tickets meant they weren't going to risk ending up stuck in the top corners, or behind one of the advertising boards positioned strategically around the stadium. The students of the academy didn't have to worry about that.

Since their school had won the National Championships last year, they were considered VIPs. Each school had a specific section set aside for them in the stands. Almost as good as the exclusive boxes bought out by the wealthiest and most powerful families, these sections ensured the students had somewhere to sit to cheer on their classmates.

Elmhurst had used her name value to secure the most desirable spot for the Elmhurst students, and the Five were more than happy to take advantage of the privilege. It meant they didn't have to rush to their seats, and could enjoy the festivities before the game.

Carson eyed a giant inflatable set up nearby. People were climbing inside wearing harnesses and were attached to a large hook with a thick bungee cord. They could then run as fast as possible and see how far they could stretch before the cord won out and snapped them backward. His eyes widened, and he walked to it, waving to the others, telling them where he was going.

"I'll go with him," Vivi said in a resigned voice. "If he snaps himself in half, I'll let you know."

Luna laughed. "Let's all go watch."

Zander rested a hand on Mia's elbow. "You guys go ahead. I'm hungry. I want to check out what the concession booths have. Mia and I will bring back some snacks."

Luna and Vivi nodded, and they headed in opposite directions. Zander drew closer to Mia as they went to the long row of concession booths. He nudged against her slightly, and Mia smiled.

"Are you excited to finally be here?" he asked.

She nodded. "It's funny, I've never been here before or done anything like this. I never even heard of Slamball until coming to the academy and meeting you guys. But somehow, it feels like it's always been a part of my life. Like I've been waiting for these championships and have been excited along with the rest of you for all these years. Does that make sense?"

"I guess it's just a part of you. You're finally learning about where you come from and the types of things you should have been doing all your life. So, now you're excited to find out new things and feel like you're a part of it all," he told her.

Before Mia could answer, something caught her attention. "Well, *he* is certainly not feeling like he's a part of it all."

She pointed at a man wandering by, and Zander looked in his direction. He was human and clearly *not* one of the locals in the know about what was happening. His wide eyes and an open mouth as he looked around said this man had no idea what was going on and was shocked by it all.

"How did he get in here?" Zander asked. "He must have wandered in with a group."

The man stopped in his tracks and stared at a group of vampires walking by. The dome protected them from the sunlight, which meant they could walk around without worrying. A few feet away, a tiny faerie spotted the man and the way he was looking at the groups around him. Knowing his presence could be a serious issue, she ran as fast as she could to talk to an official.

Hamish wasn't sure how to process everything going on around him. He was lured into the strange events happening and had followed a crowd into the carnival atmosphere. Around him, a variety of odd creatures roamed about. A gnome hurried past, carrying a massive container of popcorn. Pixies fluttered around his head, chattering to each other so fast he couldn't tell if they were speaking a different language or not. To one side, several people walked past, shifting into different forms as they went.

He was struggling to breathe and starting to feel dizzy. If he didn't know any better, he would have sworn he was living inside one of his video games.

"This can't be real. This can't be. But it is. They exist. They really do exist. All of them. They really do exist," he muttered to himself.

As he wandered and hyperventilated, the faerie reached one of the championship officials. "There's a situation," she told him. "A human is inside the dome. Not one of the locals."

"A human?" the official asked. "How did a human get inside? There are precautions set up."

"I know," the faerie said. "But something must have happened because he is inside. He's wandering around looking at the spectators."

"Something will need to be done about that."

CHAPTER FOUR

Mia felt for the human man; he was so out of place and confused. He looked frightened as if he had no idea what he was supposed to do next. At one point, he turned toward the entrance to the dome but spotted a large group of vampires coming in, followed by a troll. Gasping, he backed up several steps and whipped around. He was obviously beginning to panic.

Mia felt terrible and wanted to reassure him. "I'll be right back," she said to Zander.

"Where are you going?"

Mia wasn't supposed to be alone at any point. The Games were crawling with security, but it wasn't enough for Elmhurst and Cassia. They wanted to make sure Mia was safe, and that meant keeping an eye on her every second. She couldn't be by herself at any time, even for an instant. It wouldn't take long for someone to snatch her and disappear through a portal where they wouldn't be able to find her.

"I want to go talk to him. He looks upset, and I may be able to help him." She headed for the man, and Zander jogged to catch up with her. "Hello," she said, approaching the human carefully.

Mia didn't want to startle him. He was already going through enough and looked as if even a little thing could spook him into total panic. She paused as he turned and slid his eyes over her, scrutinizing her.

With her red hair and friendly smile, she didn't look like anyone else around him, and he relaxed slightly. "Are you… human?" he asked.

"Um," she said. "Yes, I am of human descent."

It wasn't a lie. She was just glossing over the other half of her heritage. It would help to put him at ease if he didn't have to think of her as one of the strange, unexplainable creatures startling him.

"Okay," he said, but didn't seem confident.

Mia took another step toward him and extended her hand. "My name is Mia."

He took her hand, seemingly reassured by the recognizably human gesture of shaking hands when meeting someone. "I'm Hamish," he said.

"It's nice to meet you, Hamish."

He nodded. "You, too. Can I ask you something, Mia?"

"Of course."

"What is this place?" He lowered his voice and leaned slightly toward her when he asked the question, as though he was confiding in her and didn't want anyone else to hear him.

His gaze flickered over her head, and Mia glanced over her shoulder. Zander approached slowly, staring at Hamish. She recognized the look in his eyes. It was suspicious, gauging if he could be trusted to be that close to Mia.

She looked back at Hamish and gestured at Zander. "This is my friend Zander. We're here to watch the World Slamball Championships. That's what this is. The stadium itself is at the other end of the dome."

"So, all of you…you're here to watch a game?" Hamish asked.

"It's not just a game," Zander corrected him. "It's the World Championships. It only happens once every four years. That's why there are so many people here. And of so many different species."

"The dome was put into place as a precaution to prevent humans who don't know what's going on from coming here, and getting into the area," Mia added.

"Well, it doesn't seem like it did a terribly good job, now did it?" Hamish asked.

"It's not the dome's fault you came where you weren't supposed to," Zander said.

Mia looked at him and gave a subtle shake of her head, trying to stop him. It was flattering to have the smart, handsome Seelie halfling be so protective of her and want to make sure she was safe.

At that moment, though, she felt compelled to talk to this man and make sure he was all right. She understood that look of fear and uncertainty. It was so similar to what she had been through in Shanghai when she had first started noticing the unusual creatures she'd never seen before.

She highly doubted he was on the same sort of trajectory as hers. He was too old to suddenly be discovering he had a half-fae heritage, and there didn't seem to be anyone to guide him the way Cassia had done for her.

But that didn't lessen the fear he felt. If anything, wandering into this and having no one there to help would only make it worse. Maybe she could be there for him and help him deal with what he was going through.

It wasn't just curiosity about who this man was, or a desire to comfort him that led Mia to talk to Hamish. A part of her had reached a point where she questioned everything and everyone.

After uncovering the truth about Hazel, she was more aware than ever that the greatest dangers could be lurking right there in plain sight. As much as this man might seem like a hapless human who had somehow wandered his way into the Slamball Championships, he could also be a decoy. This could be the moment in which she was manipulated into being captured. She had to be on guard and stop that from happening.

"How did you get in here?" she asked. "Why did you come?"

Hamish shook his head. "I don't know. I just felt like I had to," he told her.

"What do you mean?" Mia asked.

"I can't really explain it. I just felt this pull to this part of the island, so I came here. It's like I just needed to be here," Hamish said.

At that moment, the faerie fluttered back, bringing three officials with her. Hamish's eyes widened as they faced him, and his body tensed defensively again.

"Sir, you're going to need to come with us," one of the officials said.

Hamish looked around him as though he was seeking out a way to escape. A second official held up a hand toward him.

"You don't have to be afraid. We aren't going to do anything to hurt you. We understand you came here by mistake and are out of your element, and just want to help you," he said.

Hamish hesitated for a few seconds, but he finally nodded. Mia watched as the officials and the faerie led him away. She turned to Zander. "What are they going to do to him?" she asked. "They aren't going to hurt him, are they?"

Zander shook his head reassuringly and steered her back toward the concession booths so they could complete the mission they had been on before her detour.

"No. They aren't going to hurt him. It's undesirable, and a little inconvenient, that he's here, but not criminal. And he didn't do anything threatening or damaging. They don't have any reason to hurt him. They'll just take him to the administration offices and wipe his memory. Then they'll send him home with the implanted idea that he wants to stay there for a few days. Hopefully, that will work, and he won't come back and wander into the Games again," he told her.

As they stood in line for nachos, Mia thought about what Hamish had said before the officials arrived. After a few moments, she realized Zander was staring at her. "Is everything okay?" she asked.

"I was about to ask you the same question. It looked like you were far away for a second there," he said.

Mia gave a short laugh. "I guess I was in a way."

"What do you mean?"

"I can't stop thinking about what Hamish said when I asked him how he got into the dome. He said he didn't know how he got in or why he came here. Just that he was drawn to this area and had to come. That's how I feel," she explained.

"Called to the Games?" Zander asked.

She shook her head. "No. Not to the Games. To the mainland. Something is calling me to Scotland, but I don't know where exactly. Not yet, anyway. I've never been before, and have always thought it was such a beautiful and fascinating place to read and learn about. Maybe that's it. I'm just drawn to explore the country."

"Or maybe you want to see the faerie pools," Zander suggested.

"What are faerie pools?" she asked.

Mia had heard several people whisper about them since their arrival, but didn't know what they were talking about. Before Zander could answer, the rest of the group showed up. They were laughing and bouncing off each other as they came, and when they got close, Carson's eyes grew huge.

"You should have seen it," he gushed. "I've never experienced anything like that. It was incredible."

Mia laughed and shook her head. "I love that you have had access to magic your entire life and have recently learned to manipulate it in some exceptional ways. Yet it's the power of a massive rubber band that really invigorates you."

"Come on," Vivi said. "We've got to get in there. I don't want to still be wandering around getting to our seats when it's about to start."

They headed to the stadium and went to the reserved section. As they were passing a row of students, Mia heard one whisper to the other. "I have to go see these mystical faerie pools. My grandmother used to tell me stories about them when I was little," he said.

Mia's ears perked up, and she zeroed in on the conversation.

"So did mine," another said. "I've been wanting to see them for as long as I can remember."

"What are they?" a third asked.

"They are pools in the domain of the faeries. But it's not just regular water. It's enchanted water. That water will cure you of anything you might have wrong with you. Even cancer. Just drinking the water, or swimming in it, will make you whole again," the first answered.

"I've heard if a human gets any on them, or drinks some, it will put them in a deep sleep for over a hundred years," the second said.

"No," another who hadn't spoken yet said. "That's not how the water in the faerie pools works. I've heard even the tiniest amount can lead a human, or even a halfling, to be under the thrall of the faeries for the rest of their lives."

Mia couldn't help but shudder. After seeing what Hazel had been through while under the thrall of Jose, the thought was horrifying. She hurried to catch up with the group and poked her head in between them. Sounding like she didn't know anything was wrong, as long as she could learn more about the famous pools everyone was talking about. "What are the faerie pools?" she asked.

Vivi gave a short laugh and shook her head. "Don't listen to them. They're all wrong. The water in the faerie pools won't do anything to a halfling."

They reached their seats and settled in. Luna looked at Mia.

"They were partially right. The water does affect humans. I obviously don't know for sure, but what I've heard is the water causes humans to fall into a deep sleep. It's short, though. Just long enough for the faeries to bring them to Faerie and force them to be their slaves. Sadly, humans don't last long in Faerie," she told her.

"Is it because of the food there? Someone told me the food in Faerie harms humans," Mia said.

"No," Vivi said. "It's the beasties. They will eat the humans." She said it matter-of-factly as if it was no big deal.

Beside her, Carson laughed. "You're all wrong."

"What do *you* know about it?" Zander asked.

Carson gave a smug grin and leaned back in his seat, looking out over the playing field. "You'll see when we go there."

"So, why do we call the Russian witch team the 'Wax Weirdos' again?" Mia asked in a rare lull in the action. The game had gone back and forth, a blur of passes and slam-dunks as Elmhurst Academy and the Russian Witch Academy team played a tough and physical game.

"Well, the person who founded the school was an old witch named Wetherwax. Nicknamed Wax for short. As for the weirdoes part, well, I think that's pretty self-explanatory," Carson said. "Even for witches, the Wax Weirdos are odd. They don't do a lot of the academy events where we all get together, and they seem pretty focused on staying at home and being, well…weird."

Time was ticking away in the game, and the score had stayed fairly even. The physical brutality of the two teams was somewhat alarming, considering it was only the first match of the tournament, but Carson and Zander seemed to think it could be rougher. At one point, Vivi lamented that the Elmhurst players had yet to seriously injure anyone, and Mia laughed before realizing the girl might have been serious. Slamball was a bit more intense than anything Mia had ever seen. Even the Wushu tournaments.

In the time since her first meet though, Mia had grown to quite like the game, and now nothing compared to being in an arena rooting for her school. For a few moments, everything else melted away. The studies, the tests, the looming danger of people like Narco, the guilt of lying to her father, everything else would disappear in a haze of adrenaline and euphoria when they won. And Elmhurst won a lot. The reason they were even in the tourney was they had won their division last year.

The clock was still moving, and it seemed to tick faster every time Elmhurst had the ball. Mia found herself biting her nails. It was a habit she thought she had grown out of as a child, but anticipation and anxiety over the score brought it back. Every time one team would take the lead, the other would thunder back and tie it up. When it seemed as if Elmhurst might take a commanding lead, a mysterious collision would happen, and only half the time would someone be penalized for it. As far as Luna was concerned, and very loudly so, the judges had it in for Elmhurst from the start.

A buzzing sound alerted the players that five minutes remained in the game, and the score was still tied. Mia caught herself whispering words of encouragement under her breath, words no one could possibly hear over the roar of the crowd, not to mention the various noisemakers some of them brought. How that didn't count as contraband, Mia was still trying to figure out. The time was slipping away, yet the score remained tied, and players from each side were becoming increasingly desperate. Only seconds remained.

One of the players for the Wax Witches had the ball and took a deep bounce on the trampoline to try to slam it in. An Elmhurst player soared up to meet them, in an attempt to block. The witch panicked and threw the ball in a high arc, directly into the hands of another Elmhurst player who was jumping into just the right spot.

But before the crowd could react, another witch player shot a weak spell at him, and the Elmhurst team-member crashed to the ground, narrowly missing the trampoline with the top half of his body before landing on the mat. Whistles blew the game to a stop for injury.

A gasp filled the stadium, and the group all stood on the benches to see what was happening. Unfortunately, the people in front of Mia were extraordinarily tall, so she tugged on Zander's arm until she got his attention. He looked at her briefly and then focused on the court.

"What's going on?" Mia asked.

"A foul. It has to be. If the refs can't see that, then someone needs to do a vision spell on them," Zander said.

From between the bodies of the two tall people in front of her, Mia could almost make out the head referee who held one hand up in the air to get everyone's attention, and then made a complicated motion with her hand near her mouth, which amplified it as if it were coming through a public address system.

"Personal foul on number twenty-two. That player has been eliminated from the game."

A roar of approval from the Elmhurst side of the arena rippled through the crowd and died when it got back to the witches' side. Mia watched as medics attended to the injured boy, who looked as if he was gingerly moving his arm due to a shoulder injury. The witch being escorted off the field, however, was laughing. Not only was she unremorseful, but she was also happy.

"Elmhurst will have the ball and a free throw," the referee announced.

A general settling down of the fans meant the line of sight opened again for Mia, so she sat. This shot was for the whole game. The time on the clock was almost up, and if the Elmhurst player scored, it was likely they would win. The player, who Mia recognized as a kid named Sam, bounced the ball a few times in preparation.

Sweat dripped from his matted hair, and he eyed the hoop. On one side of him stood an Elmhurst teammate, and on his other side, a Russian witch. When Sam took the shot, they would both bounce up there, ready to grab a rebound and take another crack at it before the buzzer meant the game was over.

Sam seemed to steady himself, and Mia focused on him. The stands grew warmer, and the sound died away. Everything blurred other than Sam, the ball and the basket, which were in hyper-focus.

Mia stared at the ball as Sam lifted it to take the shot. She focused hard on the ball, on the little circular dots texturing the ball. The lines that crossed it. The logo of the league. Then she felt something else. Eyes on her.

Everything faded back into reality and real-time all at once. She turned to see Zander staring at her. He knew what was going on, and he was hoping she would do it. Like the other time, where she helped Elmhurst win, Zander was watching her to see if she did it again. Her hand shot up to her mouth, and her eyes widened in shock as Sam made his move.

Zander slid over to her as the ball hit the rim and bounced up in the air. Both of the other players jumped to get near it, but the arc of the bounce took it straight up before it fell ever so slightly toward Mark, an Elmhurst team-member, who grabbed it and slammed it in with one mighty movement. Elmhurst had scored.

The roar of the crowd was deafening, and all around them, people were on their feet, high-fiving, and shouting. But Zander and Mia sat next to each other, his hand moving to touch her back.

"Are you all right?" he asked.

"Yes, I'm fine. I just realized what you meant last year."

"Shhh," Zander said. "Let's discuss all that later, okay?"

Mia nodded, and Zander offered her his hand. She took it and stood with him, just in time for Luna to turn around, a mask of excitement on her face and a squeal coming from deep within her.

"We did it," Luna shouted and wrapped Mia up in a tight hug.

"I know, it was so awesome," Mia responded. It was awesome. But something was bugging her.

"Now *that* was a pro-level move," exclaimed Carson. "But how in the hell did Mark and Sam pull that off? There's no way they could do that."

"Well, Sam missed the shot," Vivi said. "It was all Mark there. And Mark is better than you give him credit for."

"Please," Carson argued. "I've seen that kid miss dunks when he had no defenders. And that was the Weirdoes' best defender he dunked on. No way."

"Well, you saw it happen, Carson," Luna interrupted. "We won!"

Zander turned his head slightly to look at Mia. His eyebrow arched up questioningly. Mia shook her head firmly and smiled. It wasn't her.

"Well, either by luck or by talent, we won," Carson said. "And now we move on to the next game, and the Weirdo's are toast. I say we celebrate. Anybody else for a stroll through the faerie pools?"

"I don't think that's a good idea." Zander sounded disappointed as he looked at his watch. "It's getting late, and we still have class tonight."

"We could head over there this weekend, though," Luna suggested.

"Not a bad idea," Zander said. "Everybody in agreement?"

Nods of approval rounded the group, and they gathered their things for the trek back home. Once through the portal and back on campus, the group split off in different directions to prepare for their classes. Zander sidled up to Mia, though, and she slowed to give them a little space to talk alone.

"So that wasn't you?" Zander asked, his voice above a hoarse whisper.

"No, but you were right. I did manipulate the game last year. Not on purpose. It almost happened again tonight, but since I have a better handle on what magic feels like leaving my body, I was able to stop it. I could feel it building up when Sam was getting ready to toss the free throw. I wanted him to make the shot so badly. But I didn't know that other people could redirect the ball, and when he actually shot the ball, I had turned my attention to you."

"I saw," he said, with the hint of a smile. "But Carson has a point. That was a pro-level rebound and dunk by Mark. It was so smooth, so slick and perfectly timed, it just didn't feel like it was real."

Mia nodded.

"Hey, maybe they just worked on rebounds a lot this summer," Zander continued, his voice a little louder now, and seeming to break some of the tension in the conversation.

"Yeah, maybe," Mia said. "I saw them practicing an awful lot when we first got back to school."

"Maybe that's it, then," Zander said, his hands falling to his sides with a shrug.

"You don't seem so sure," Mia said.

"Well, let's suppose something *was* up. You didn't do it. And there are magical protections to keep players and fans from one side hexing the other. None of the other students can do it, for sure, so who does that leave? A fae in the audience? Or maybe a witch?"

"Why would a witch want their own team to lose?" Mia asked, confused.

"Exactly, it doesn't make sense. That brings us back to a fae. It had to be a fae, but who was it?"

Mia shook her head. With a shrug, Zander indicated he was as lost as she was. A few moments later, they said goodbye, and Mia stood alone under the setting sun, the oranges and reds painted across the sky calming her. She pulled her jacket around her tighter, noting with delight that some of the chill from Scotland had followed her home. Still, the pull to go back was strong, and she longed for tomorrow when there might be a chance to go again.

Zander was right. Something had happened tonight, and she didn't know what. But Mark making that play, so easily, and so perfectly timed, was a bit of a stretch. But who would have the motive, the ability, and the stealth, to pull it off? That was a mystery Mia couldn't figure out, but she did know Elmhurst was going to play at least one more game. And now, Mia knew what to look for.

CHAPTER SIX

Cassia sat back in the large leather chair in Elmhurst's office. It was stiff and hard, designed more for making students who had broken the rules feel even more anxious than it was for comfort, but she still tried to relax. She didn't give herself much time to sit anymore. If she wasn't eating or sleeping, she kept herself moving.

She had to keep looking, keep searching for the people who posed such a tremendous threat to her young halfling ward. Spending time with Mia over the summer had been wonderful, and had given them the chance to grow closer. It made the fae bounty hunter more devoted to ensuring Mia didn't fall into the wrong hands and get hurt. Cassia was exhausted and frustrated, but it wasn't stopping her.

"There's been no sign of him?" Elmhurst asked from her seat on the other side of the desk.

Cassia shook her head. "No. I haven't seen or heard anything from Narco in all the time I've been searching. It's worrying me."

"But, that's a good thing, isn't it?" the headmistress asked.

"It's good that he hasn't been around Mia, and hasn't tried to attack her. But it also means we haven't been able to stop him. If he's somewhere in hiding, staying away from her and from us, that's fine. The longer he stays away from her, the better. But if he is on the move, we may not see him coming. He has countless followers, and any of them could be helping to hide his tracks. They could be working to disguise what he's doing and where he is, so we don't know what to expect. How are we supposed to effectively protect Mia from an attack if we don't see it coming?" Cassia said.

"I don't think that's something you need to be worried about," Elmhurst assured her. "I know you're concerned about Mia, and you want to make sure she stays safe. That's the top priority for all of us, of course. But I have confidence in you and your associates. I know you'll be able to find Narco before he can get to Mia. And, besides that, I have full faith in Mia as well. I believe she and her friends can protect themselves. She is extraordinary, Cassia. Even more than you might understand. In the last few months, they have really devoted themselves to their work, and have come a long way. Their practice is paying off more every single day. It's becoming much easier for Mia to call on her powers, and to control them."

"Really?" Cassia asked.

"They haven't had a natural disaster since last semester. Not even a small windstorm. No fires. No floods. She hasn't accidentally hurt anyone. They have even managed to obtain the Power of 5 successfully on multiple occasions. They don't even have to do grade-school level spells anymore. Mia has not only managed to go from having no understanding of her powers and no skills to reach her grade-level abilities, to a place well beyond all expectations. I've even found her tutoring others in her grade to help them accomplish skills and spells they're struggling with. She will only keep growing stronger. I know she'll be able to handle herself," Elmhurst told her.

On the other side of campus, Mia, Zander, Luna, Carson, and Vivi, chatted as they walked to the library. The class they had inside the library was small and exclusive, one of the several invitation-only sessions designed for those in their senior year. The Five had been invited into one of these special classes solely for them to practice and study together.

As they approached the library, they heard Dan and Steve grumbling between themselves on their daytime perches. They fussed and groaned, lamenting at having to stay still all day long.

"It's not fair," Dan said. "The days are so much longer during the summer. We have to sit here all day, even when the sun is up for hours longer."

"I know," Steve agreed. "And that means the night hours are shorter, so we don't get as much time to be free. The rules should change with the time of year."

"But that would mean you would have to stay in place during the winter months when there are longer dark hours," Dan said. "We should be grateful that winter's coming, and the days are getting shorter."

"And what about cloudy weather and rain?" Steve demanded, ignoring Dan's comment.

"What about them?" Dan asked.

"They blot out a lot of the sunlight. They make it almost as dark as when it's nighttime. But do we get to get off our platforms when that's happening? No. We have to just stay here and get wet and be miserable," Steve snapped.

"The clouds aren't that bad. At least that means we don't have glare in our eyes," Dan tried to tell him.

"Look, I can resolve this for both of you." Vivi moved closer to both of them. "If you're tired of the weather, I can give Steve a burst of sunshine. And, Dan, I can make a cloud over just you. That way, both of you can have something different, and you won't have to complain."

Both gargoyles gasped. They turned their attention to her.

"Get bent!" Steve shouted.

"Yeah, Vivi, make like a tree and leave!" Dan joined in.

"Scram before I give you a knuckle sandwich!" Steve said.

"We don't need your kind of riffraff around here."

"You're nothing more than a dingleberry!" Steve shouted, and Dan burst into raucous laughter.

If he hadn't been attached to his pedestal, Dan would have tumbled backward with the intensity of his laughter. But Vivi merely stared at them in confusion. She was accustomed to them hurling insults and slang from the middle of the last century at them, but dingleberry was a new one. She glanced back at the group, but they shrugged. None of them had any answer for her.

"What are you talking about?" she asked. "What is a dingleberry?"

The gargoyles almost couldn't get themselves under control, but Dan finally managed to calm his laughter down enough to string words together. "You know those little poop balls that hang onto the hair around an animal's butthole?" he exclaimed. He barely got the words out of his mouth before bursting into laughter again.

Vivi's face grew hot and red, and she clenched her hands into tight fists at her sides. Anger and humiliation rushed up inside her, stinging the back of her neck.

"I really hope both of you are looking forward to a wet school year. I'm going to start a thunderstorm over both of you that no one can stop. As long as you're standing on those pedestals, it's going to be raining on you," she threatened.

Mia walked up beside her. "You know, Vivi, if you don't want the gargoyles mad at you, you really shouldn't tease them." She turned to the gargoyles. "You guys know she wouldn't actually do any of that to you, right?"

The stone statues blustered and stuttered, not ready to admit the Unseelie girl wouldn't carry out her threat.

"You've seen her," Dan said.

"You know the kinds of things she's done to us," Steve pointed out.

"Now, come on, guys. Vivi wouldn't do that to you without provocation," Mia added.

Behind her, Carson, Zander, and Luna laughed. Mia shot a glare over her shoulder. The three did their best to stifle their amusement and pull themselves together. Luna held her hand over her mouth, and Zander looked at his feet, but his shoulders were shaking.

Mia turned to the gargoyles. "Guys?" she asked.

"All right," Dan said grudgingly. "You're right."

"We'll just ignore her," Steve agreed.

Out of nowhere, Cinder zipped at Vivi's head. The little pixie was far from convinced of Vivi's innocence. "You better not hurt Dan and Steve!" she yelled, her voice a high-pitched screech

She zoomed around Vivi in a fast whirlwind, wagging one little finger at her. Just as she flew past her head again, Cinder sneezed. The tips of Vivi's hair caught fire. Luna gasped and ran to help before the other halfling went up in flames.

Before she could get there, Steve reached inside himself. Several weeks before, during one of the rare summer rains, he had opened his mouth—one of the few things he could still move while stuck on his pedestal—and had let it fill with water. He'd been holding it in case Vivi ever decided to play another practical joke on them again.

He hadn't planned on needing to use it to save her. But he did, dousing her with the water and putting out the sizzling flames. Vivi's hands balled up again, and she released an exasperated, infuriated sound, somewhere between a scream and a growl.

"How dare you?" she shouted, stomping her feet.

"Hey, I saved your hair by putting out the fire as quickly as I could," Steve pointed out. "You should be thanking me."

Vivi drew in a breath and stalked toward the dorms without saying another word. The other four exchanged glances. They knew she wouldn't be coming back any time soon. There was a brief moment when Mia and Luna considered following her, but it wouldn't do any good. Besides, they needed to go to class. Vivi brought these things on herself.

With as much as she messed with the gargoyles—and everyone else for that matter—eventually, it was going to come back on her. She should be happy it was something as simple as some water on her head.

They entered the class as the teacher was beginning her lecture. She looked at the four halflings. "Where's Vivi?"

"She had to go back to the dorm," Zander told her.

"There was an incident with Dan and Steve," Mia explained. "And Cinder."

The teacher looked at Luna for more information. "Cinder was worried about the gargoyles, and accidentally sneezed on Vivi's head, which set her hair on fire, so Steve dumped water on her head."

The teacher's gaze moved to Carson.

"Oh," he said, not expecting to need to add anything.

"It started because they called her a poop ball," Mia said.

The class erupted into laughter as they went to their seats. Carson leaned toward Mia.

"You should have made something up," he whispered. "This is going to make Vivi mad at you."

"Isn't she always mad at me, anyway?" Mia sighed.

"You're the one who told the class they called her a poop ball," Zander pointed out. "That probably isn't going to help."

Near the end of class, the teacher was still droning on about the same lecture she gave during the last session, trying to get some of the stragglers to understand. Luna moved closer to the group.

"I think we should start planning our trip to the Isle of Skye so we can learn more about the faeries and their pools," she whispered.

"I think we need to search the library for the truth about the water first," Zander suggested. "I want to know what we're getting ourselves into before we just go."

"I think that's a fantastic idea, Zander," the teacher said, overhearing their conversation. "In keeping with the spirit of the Slamball Championships, I'm assigning all of you a report on Scotland. I want you to research how its history is intertwined with the fae and other supernatural elements. You're all dismissed."

Mia shrugged as she packed her bag. "I think the assignment is going to be interesting. We can find all the local lore and cross-reference those with the fae library. We can find out which stories are real. Or, at least as close to real as they get."

As they left the class area, she again felt the tug toward Scotland, and maybe even to the faerie pools.

CHAPTER SEVEN

"F"un assignment, huh?" Zander said, coming around the corner of a bookshelf and surprising Mia, who was deep into a chapter of a book.

She had grabbed the copy off the shelf at random, hoping anything with the words "Scotland" and "Faerie" in it might shed some light on both their assignment and the mysterious pool in Skye. A chapter had caught her attention, and she had been lost in a world of vampire lore when Zander's head popped into her peripheral vision, startling her so much she almost dropped the book.

"It is. It's complicated, though," she responded.

That analysis was growing more obvious the longer she worked on the project. The report they needed to do was on a broad subject. Researching the history of Scotland, and how it intertwined with the history of the fae and other supernatural creatures, was a long, long story, as she was finding out.

As interesting as it might be to read about the local lore with a thought to possibly exploring some of it during the Games, it still represented a challenge as a project. Especially since Vivi had checked out so far.

Usually, when Zander interrupted her thought process, Mia was all too willing to drop whatever it was and follow his lead. Yet, this time, her eyes returned to the page, as though magnetized. It was hard to let go of the world she was learning about, and the tug on her heartstrings to Scotland, and on her mind to the faerie pools, was strong.

Mia fought the urge to sit cross-legged in the aisle and read until the end of the class time. She shut the book a bit harder than she meant to and looked up at Zander, who was staring at her expectantly.

"Sorry," Mia said, shaking off the spell the book had put her under.

"So, Carson and Luna have wandered off into the lower level of the archives. We only have a few minutes left in class, so I was going to head down to them and see if they found anything. Want to come?"

"Sure." Mia tucked the book under her arm and picked up her bag.

They went deep into the library, which seemed to stretch on for miles. From what Mia understood, it actually did in a way. The building itself was so infused with magic that temporal holes in reality had been created in certain areas, allowing for exploitation by those who knew how to bend and shape forces in on themselves.

While on the outside, the library was only one large domed building, on the inside it was at least four times that size, and that was before counting the stairs leading underground to the second and third floors. The bottom floor was forbidden to anyone except teachers, professors, and visiting alumni, along with students who had a special pass.

Mia often wondered what magical texts were kept there. She had heard rumors of books that were sentient and needed to be caged since horrible creatures and terrible spells had been trapped inside them.

Though they were still on the first floor, Carson and Luna had gone deep into the stacks to a place Mia had never been before. Though she tried to keep up with the categories on the shelves, she was soon lost, and dependent on Zander to guide her.

He had spent far more time in the library than any of them. Thankfully, he seemed quite confident in where they were going. They rounded a particularly odd sculpture, surrounded by old-looking books. Luna and Carson appeared in the distance, and Mia walked more confidently toward them. When they looked up and saw her, Carson's eyes shot to his watch, and panic crossed his face.

"Crickets! We only have five minutes left, and I have to get across campus for my next class. We've got to get out of here," Carson said.

Zander checked his watch too. Both he and Carson had the same class.

"Well, that was a waste of my time then," said a voice from behind Mia. She turned to Vivi, who looked less frazzled, her hair an inch or two shorter. "I'll just take this." She reached into the display with the statue and grabbed a particularly old book.

"Wait, what book is that?" Luna asked, suddenly intrigued. She went to Vivi, who held it out, turning it this way and that.

"I don't know, just something old as dirt. Probably boring too," Vivi said.

"That's bound with leather." Carson came up behind Luna.

They were all crowding around Vivi, staring down at the book. Even Vivi was starting to look more interested. Mia was close now, and she reached out to touch the cover.

The leather felt warm and smooth, like a high-backed chair in a fancy office. But old. She couldn't properly describe it, it just felt *old*. Older than old. Ancient. Like it was an artifact from another time.

"It looks like animal skin. They used to print them on animal skin centuries ago, but books that old are usually locked up in the special reference section. What is that doing out here?" said Luna, mesmerized.

"Maybe it's some kind of special edition reprint or something," Zander suggested.

"Yeah, because that's a thing," mocked Vivi. "I can't tell you about all those volumes of Ancient Texts of the Babylonian Fae that I got with special gold binding. My father joined one of those clubs where you can buy one for full price, and get a hundred others for a penny apiece."

"Then what in Faerie is it doing up here?" Carson asked.

"I don't know, but it's glowing," Zander said.

He was right. A small yellowish gleam had begun to emanate from the leather cover where Mia had placed her hand. The light was cold and silky, like putting on lotion, and when Vivi looked down, the glow had grown brighter and wider and was threatening to cover her hands.

She screamed and dropped the book. "What is that, what is that, what is that?"

Vivi ran for cover behind Carson, shaking her hands as if trying to get water off them. They all stared at the book where it now sat on the ground, unmoving. It was almost mocking in how normal it looked, lying there on the ground—as though the glowing had been an illusion.

"What do we do now?" Carson muttered.

Vivi was clutching the back of his shirt, peering over his shoulder, prepared to duck at the first sign of sentience displayed by the book.

"Someone has to pick it up," Zander said.

Various non-committal sounds came from Carson and Vivi. Luna, for her part, stood stock still. She was obviously interested in the book and was fighting the dual truths. A book that could harm her shouldn't possibly be where she could access it, and this book was most certainly not meant to be where she was.

"I'll do it." Mia had been expecting an outcry. When none came, she knelt to pick the book up, noting that, for what it was worth, *she* was being the brave one right now.

Or the stupid one. Most likely the stupid one.

As she wrapped her hands around the book, the glow returned, and she dropped it. She looked at the others and saw the curiosity mixed with mild panic on the faces of her friends.

On the one hand, the book had to be returned to where it belonged, and it certainly wasn't here. On the other, if this book belonged down on the third floor of the library, then it contained forbidden knowledge and was, therefore, what Mia wanted to see.

In spite of her own better judgment, she snatched the book up again and threw it open to a random page.

"Well?" said Vivi from just above Carson's shoulder.

"Is it full of ancient spells?" Zander asked.

"Or tales of the bloodlust of the Elder Ones?" Luna whispered. Zander, Vivi, and Carson all turned to her slowly, staring. "What? The Elder Ones were well known for having bloodlust. Do you guys not pay attention in class?"

But Mia didn't hear them. She was lost in the story, taking it in as if she were breathing in the words rather than reading them, and they became part of her, intertwining with her DNA with every letter. The story was intoxicating, and she stood transfixed until she felt Zander's hands on her shoulders as he was shaking her.

"Mmm-wha?" she said, coming out of her trance.

"Are you okay? What does the book say?" Zander asked.

Carson and Vivi had sat down at some point, Carson apparently forgoing his next class and risking punishment.

"I'm fine. Really." Mia paused and then looked at the book again. Just like the book about Scotland, this one had its own gravitational pull, and she had to force her eyes up to look into Zander's. "It's about a princess. A fae princess lost in the human realm. It's an ancient story, well before the last king and queen of faerie. Her name was Caledona. Princess Caledona."

She looked between the faces of the group and saw no recognition. No one had ever heard that name. Mia cleared her throat to go on, forcing herself not to look at the book again.

"She was brought up by the Picts. They thought she was the child of one of the local deities, but she wasn't. However, she helped them. Her powers let her make the crops grow, and the forests larger. She could help animals and bewitch men to do anything she wanted them to."

"Now we're talking. I could go for some men bewitching," Vivi said, snickering.

"She was most likely a fae child left behind," Zander suggested. "Maybe even a halfling. For a Pict, she would seem like a goddess. Especially considering that, to other species, fae all have an innate beauty. Even halflings."

CHAPTER EIGHT

"Will you shut up?" Vivi said, slapping Zander on the arm.

"Did you just hit me?" Zander asked incredulously.

"Yeah, and I'll do it again if you don't zip it. For once in her life, Mia has something interesting to say that has nothing to do with her setting everything on fire, or not being able to do a basic spell. So I, for one, would like to hear it."

"Thank you for that," Mia interrupted. Her stony expression toward Vivi was met with a similarly hard glare, and Mia decided to just move past it. Sitting in one of the ubiquitous chairs in the library, she thumbed through a couple of pages, her mouth moving with the words. "Okay, so this is interesting."

"Just get on with it, please," Vivi pleaded. Carson sat cross-legged in front of Mia, and Zander joined him. Luna followed suit, leaving only Vivi standing. She huffed loudly, looking at the rest of the group before plopping down herself. "Go on, tell us a story, you've got the spotlight, just like always."

Ignoring her, Mia cleared her throat.

"In the time of Princess Caledona, it was known there was no other creature like her under the stars," she read. "Thusly the natives of the land, the Picts, did worship her and made her their *bana-phrionnsa*, as the locals even now call her, a Gaelic word for 'princess.' There were many battles in which the Picts were dominant with her at their side. They held off more sophisticated and well-appointed armies twice their size, with their own simple archers and soldiers bearing only rocks and clubs. Stories remain of her ability to bend the sky and tame the land at will, to create light and fire from her hands. There was a battle the locals called 'The War of the Broken Water,' which solidified the legend near the beginning of her time.

"Though she was barely an adult, she came to the aid of her adopted people, joining them on the battle lines as an invader from the east raided them. The battlefield was littered with the bodies of many of the Picts, the broken and the dead, but with a movement of her hand, Princess Caledona brought forth the power of water in multiple forms. First, heavy snow fell, though it was the middle of the warm season, and it buried the enemy where they stood. Then she called upon the waters of the lakes, which filled the valley and became ice. The invaders were frozen in the water, and there perished of the cold. When all of the invaders, save two, had died, she unfroze the lake and allowed them to live if they would go back to their people with the warning that the Picts were under her protection. They did as she asked and were never seen there again.

"For every battle the Picts fought with her by their side, the Picts would find themselves victorious, against insurmountable odds. She could call down the rains and the fires of the Earth. Even the strong winds would bend to her will, and destroy the enemies of their tribe. Yet, with this power, they never tried to conquer more land or aggress against anyone else. They preferred to be left alone, to be left in the land their fathers settled. But the march of the Romans was soon at hand, and thus they faced enemies for many of their days.

"And so it went that Princess Caledona was laid to rest, having passed of nothing worse than the effect of age, the Roman armies were at their doorstep. Without her, the Picts fought to nearly the last man but succumbed to the armor and steel of the Roman armies. Within a

matter of years, Romans, invaders from Ireland, and southern Scots claimed the land of the Picts and sent them away, most to the grave. Those who were left had to flee their land and live as wanderers. Yet, her story remains, and her name is spoken of in many languages, but only in whispers, and by those who fear a return of the Princess of the Picts, and the revenge she could cast on the world."

When the words stopped echoing in the chamber of the library, as one, the group felt the tension release. As Mia had read from the book, it was as though the room had grown smaller and warmer, and the outside world had lost focus.

Mia's voice grew in strength and tone, and she had commanded their attention. It was as if something within her had risen to the surface when the name of the Pict Princess was mentioned, and Vivi especially was intrigued. She eyed the book, watching intently as Mia closed it and lay it on her lap.

"Wow," Zander said, finally breaking the silence.

"Wow," Carson agreed.

"Do you think—" Mia began, then shrugged the thought away. But the question was too strong, the implication too large for her to ignore. "Do you think she could be an ancestor of mine?"

Mia looked at Zander, who gave a shrug and shook his head. Carson repeated the motion and brushed his hand through his hair. Vivi's eyes closed as she shook her head confidently. Only Luna didn't move. They all turned to her, and she shrugged, sighing.

"We don't know. We can't really. Not without knowing more about her heritage. I mean, you didn't even know you were a halfling, so we don't know that much about you. But most likely, Princess Caledona was the first-ever halfling," Luna said, finally.

"I need to know more about where I really come from," Mia said firmly. "I need to get to the bottom of this anyway, and this... something about this story, and the way I feel every time I think about Scotland—"

"You can't just go around telling people, though," Carson said.

"Maybe you can talk to Cassia. Or Elmhurst. But nobody else. It's way too dangerous."

The group jumped to their feet and came closer to Mia. They were looking directly at her, but Vivi's eyes were somewhere else. They were on the book. Luna nudged her.

Vivi snapped her head toward Luna and glared at her. "What?" she asked.

"You haven't said anything about who Mia really is, have you?" Luna asked, a sharper tone than normal in her voice. "Not to anyone, right?"

"Ha!" Vivi exclaimed, moving back a half-step. "Why in the world would I do that? Not only would it get us *all* in hot water, but this is—I'll say it slowly, so you'll all understand—the single dumbest thing I have ever heard. I mean, look at her. It's Mia. Our darling, rather inept Mia, some sort of lost princess? Come on. Why would I spread gossip that makes someone else look good, if it has no benefit to me? It would make me look dumber than a box of rocks, anyway."

"True, you wouldn't want anyone else to be elevated above you, so I guess Mia's probably safe," Luna responded. This elicited a laugh from the boys and Mia, and finally, Vivi, who shook her head, smiling.

"Yeah, that's the problem. Me and my big ol' ego. Why would I say something to make Mia look good? Why wouldn't I just spread the rumor about myself? See? Dumb," Vivi replied.

Luna nodded and turned to Carson, who was muttering something about the class he was now hopelessly late for, and Vivi's attention left the conversation. Her eyes returned to the book, and they crawled over it hungrily. She needed that book, and she needed to see if her theory was right. Zander would never go for it, and neither would Carson, but if she could get the book back to her room, maybe, just maybe she could find out for herself.

"You should put that back," Zander said, breaking Vivi's

concentration. She looked at him as he knelt and reached for the book. "May I?" he asked Mia, who nodded. He took the book and held it out to Vivi. "Since you're the one who found it, you should be able to figure out where it was placed and put it back there. Last thing we need is someone saying we broke into the archives and stole a restricted book. Here."

Vivi fought to keep her hands from shaking as she took the book from Zander. She wanted to snatch it and run back to her room. She wanted to find out right here, right now. She wanted to clear all this up before she drew another breath, but she had to play it cool. Zander was a good kid and was growing into a good man, but he was a stickler for rules. She needed to get him away before she could do anything.

"No problem," she said, blinking quite a few more times than necessary in an attempt to appeal with her feminine sensibilities.

"Do you have something stuck in your eye?" Zander asked quietly.

The smile, which had turned upward in an attempt to diffuse, now vanished from her face as she reeled from the insult. She turned her back on him and went to the display where she had found the book. The rest of the group joined her, and she feigned a critical examination of the arrangement, as though she were trying to figure out exactly how the book had been laid.

"We're going to head out. See you back at the room?" Luna asked.

"Yeah, I'll be right behind you. I just want to make sure this is perfect," Vivi said, placing the book on top of a stack of others, turning it a few times as if she was trying to get the angle right.

When the group was several steps away, she glanced at them to gauge the direction of their attention, and deciding they were all looking elsewhere, she stuffed the book in her bag and threw it over her shoulders. As soon as they rounded a large bookcase and could no longer see her, she rushed after them.

CHAPTER NINE

Mia was on edge throughout the walk from the library to the dorm. She had seen Vivi sneak the book into her bag, and was worried someone was going to catch the Five in the act.

Though there weren't any signs or anything that expressly said they weren't allowed to take the books out of that section of the library, she didn't think it took much of a stretch of the imagination to understand the point.

The books were kept in a section far away from everything else, and the barcode that should have been on the back of the book was missing. Mia had used the restricted-circulation research-books at the library in her human high school and knew how intense the librarians could be about those books staying safe. And those hadn't been bound in animal skin that glowed.

"Aren't you going to get into trouble if someone finds out you have that?" she asked, eyeing the book as Vivi curled up onto her bed to look at it.

The dark-haired girl was startled, then looked at Mia with an expression of false innocence. "Why would you think that? Would I ever do anything against the rules?" she asked.

Mia gave her an unconvinced glare. "Yes. Without thinking twice about it. But that's not the point. I'm thinking more along the lines of the fact that the book was in a hidden section of the library I didn't even know existed. And it doesn't exactly look like the rest of the books there. Besides, you didn't check it out. I wouldn't think you would need to smuggle a book out of the library if you were allowed to take it with you," Mia pointed out.

"All right. So I'm not technically allowed to have this book out of the non-circulating section of the library," Vivi said.

"I don't think that's a technicality. I think that's just a rule. What are you going to do if they figure out it was you?"

"How are they going to figure that out?" Vivi asked.

"I don't know. Magic detectors?"

Luna laughed. "They don't have magic detectors the way they have metal detectors in the human world."

"It's going to be fine," Vivi assured her. "No one is going to go looking for this musty old book. And even if they do, there's no way they are going to figure out I took it."

"And if they do?" Mia asked.

"I'll blame it on you," she said matter-of-factly, shrugging as she looked at the book again.

"What?" Mia snapped.

"I'll just tell them you were so enthusiastic about the project you wanted to do extra research. And since you are not as knowledgeable and well-versed about the school as we are, you didn't know you weren't allowed to take those books out. You put it in your backpack, and we didn't know you had it until we came back to the dorm and saw you with it," Vivi said.

Mia stared back at her for a few seconds and blinked. "You can't be serious."

"She's not," Luna said.

"But even if I was, it's not like you'd get in any trouble. You get away with everything around here," Vivi pointed out.

"That's not exactly true," Mia said.

"It doesn't matter. You're not going to get in any trouble because no one is going to find out."

"Why did you take it anyway?" Luna asked. "I thought you didn't believe Mia was descended from Princess Caledona."

"I don't. But I can't help but notice that this book seems to react to her." She held the book out toward Mia. "It illuminated when you touched it. Maybe there's a special message in it for you."

Mia took the book. Just as it did before, the book gave off a glow when she touched it. She didn't know what it meant, but it stirred something inside her.

"What kind of message could it have?" she asked. "No words are showing up on it, or anything. I don't think I see anything in it that you don't."

"Maybe it's not just that you touch it," Vivi said. "Maybe the illumination is just pointing out that there is something special about you and the book combined. We have to do something else to make it reveal itself."

"Like what?" Luna asked.

Vivi thought for a few seconds before her eyes widened. "Blood."

"Excuse me?" Mia asked.

"Blood," Vivi said again.

"I was afraid that's what you said," Mia said.

"What do you mean?" Luna asked. "Why are you talking about blood?"

"Maybe the book will respond to her blood. If there really is something special about Mia, if she really is royal, then it is literally in her blood. That could be what it takes to reveal the meaning of the book."

"And how exactly do you suggest we find something like that out?" Mia asked.

Vivi shrugged nonchalantly. "I have a knife. We can just cut your hand and collect some of the blood. We'll put it on the book and see what, if anything, it does to it."

Mia and Luna laughed, shaking their heads at the absurd suggestion. Vivi looked back at them with a blank look on her face, then crawled to the edge of her bed. She opened the drawer of her nightstand, reached in, and pulled out what looked like a dagger. The laughter instantly died, and a painful lump formed in Mia's throat when she realized Vivi was serious. She recoiled from Vivi and stared wide-eyed at Luna.

"Vivi, be serious," Luna said.

"I am." Vivi presented the knife. "Come on. It won't be deep. Just big enough to get some blood. I'm not asking for a full-on deluge or anything. A few drops should be enough for the book to reveal its secrets if there are any. I'll do it in the heel of your hand. You'll barely feel it." She waited for an acknowledgment. "Okay, you can do it yourself then. That might make it easier for you. Just a quick cut, and it will be over."

"Absolutely not," Mia said. "I don't care what your theory is. I'm not going to slice open my hand to test it out."

Vivi sighed. "Fine. It was just a thought." She put the knife back in the drawer and closed it.

"Thank you," Mia said.

"You know, using blood in a situation like this really isn't all that strange," Vivi said. "At least, it didn't used to be."

"You've got to be kidding me," Mia snapped. "I'm not going to change my mind, Vivi. You're not going to convince me."

"Actually, she's right," Luna offered. "Not that I condone her suggestion or anything, but the ancient fae were into a lot of really strange stuff. Blood spells weren't out of the question."

"See?" Vivi asked. "It's legitimate. Some magic is designed to only work for a very specific person. And the only way to prove you are that person is to offer some of your blood."

"Yes, Vivi, but that was more than two thousand years ago," Luna said. "I don't really think those kinds of things apply anymore. It could be really dangerous. Not just cutting Mia, which has its own problems, but what the blood might do to the book. We have no real idea why the book illuminates when she touches it, or what that might mean. We can't do something as drastic as put her blood on the book without having someone more knowledgeable and skilled with us. It could be really dangerous."

"Yeah, you said that," Vivi pointed out. "Come on, Mia. Aren't you just a little bit curious about what might happen?"

Mia shook her head. "I don't want to do it. I'm not familiar with anything like this, and I don't feel comfortable trying it."

She held the book out to Vivi, who sighed and took it. "All right. We won't," she said, putting the book away.

The three girls were so invested in their conversation that they didn't notice they weren't the only ones in their dorm room. A little creature flitted around, paying close attention to everything they were saying. She took it all in, listening to their words, watching the way they looked at each other.

Cinder listened carefully to the girls talking about the book, and to Vivi trying to convince them to do the blood spell. There was so much more to all of this than they knew. She knew more, but she wasn't going to say anything to them. She didn't want to come right out and reveal everything she knew. At the same time, Mia deserved to know.

The little pixie tossed the situation around in her head. She debated the importance of telling Mia and making sure she understood. Finally, she decided she would tell Mia, but not the others. They shouldn't know. At least, not yet.

That meant she needed to watch Mia and find a time when she wasn't surrounded by the other halflings so she could talk to her. Once it was just the two of them, Cinder would tell her what she knew.

CHAPTER TEN

Classes always seemed to take longer on Fridays. By the time she had completed her third month at the academy, Mia was all but convinced that was by design. She figured the teachers sometimes didn't accomplish enough during the week and didn't want to drag their lesson plans and projects into the next week.

Rather than cutting the amount of work they had for the students short, they used magic to extend the lessons on Friday without the clock actually showing the minutes passing. Mia hadn't shared that particular theory with any of the others, but it came back to mind every single week of the school year.

This Friday seemed especially long and tiresome. It was as though the teacher knew they were all distracted by The Games and weren't going to be paying much attention to their schoolwork until the championships were over. She wanted to stuff as much information as she possibly could into this week of classes before releasing them into the weekend.

By the time the lesson ended, Mia felt like she had been sitting in that same class for days. She slung her backpack over her shoulder and dragged herself from the classroom to meet with the others.

Zander looked energetic and excited as he joined her.

"What are you so happy about?" she asked. "Weren't we in the same class?"

Zander laughed. "Yes. But I'm still in a good mood."

"You're always in a good mood," Carson said, sounding as exhausted as Mia felt when he walked up to them. "It's kind of disgusting."

Zander shot him a look of mock anger. "Be nice, or I won't take you with me," he said. His voice was almost sing-songy as if he was baiting them. But it worked.

"Take us where?" Vivi asked.

"It's Friday, isn't it?" Zander asked. "I think it's time for some fun. And it just so happens I made us reservations."

"Reservations?" Mia asked.

"On the Isle of Skye. I secured a site for us to camp for the weekend. That way, we don't have to come back here every night. It will save us a lot of hassle, and we'll be able to experience more of the fun. There are two tents there waiting for us, and I have all the rest of the gear we'll need in my dorm room. My father had it delivered to me today," Zander announced.

His extremely wealthy human father always ensured that Zander had what he wanted and needed. This was especially true when his son accomplished something impressive at school. Considering how rapidly Zander and the Five were progressing in their studies and their skills, this was frequent. He was very proud of his son, and with his tremendously powerful position working for the fae, he earned the money and privilege to provide for Zander.

It didn't surprise Mia that Zander would do everything he could to make sure their experience with The Games was the best it could be. But she also knew Zander still longed to know his mother, the fae woman who had abandoned him at birth. It was only natural that he would want to know why she didn't want to be a part of his life.

"Camping? You made us reservations to go camping at the games?" Mia asked.

"Count me in!" Cinder appeared unexpectedly and startled the group.

Zander smiled. "Of course, you're always included, squirt."

Cinder's eyes narrowed, and she clenched her fists against her sides. "I'm warning you."

"All right, knock it off, you two." Mia chuckled and looked at the expression on Carson's face, hoping he wasn't upset about Cinder tagging along. She liked having her pixie friend along with them. Plus, since she was related to the faeries who guarded the pools, Mia believed it would be helpful having her along.

Carson's mouth fell open. "Isn't that against the rules?"

Cinder crossed her arms over her chest and hmphed. "I'm allowed to go anywhere I want."

Mia thought Cinder's pouty face was cute and had to hold back a giggle. "Cinder, I think he's asking about us camping for the weekend."

"Oh, well. Yeah. I think that might be against the rules. You should probably get permission from Elmhurst first." Cinder nodded and flew away from the group in order to watch them all. She wasn't sure what they were up to, but she would keep an eye on them and do her best to protect Mia. Even if that meant she had to protect the girl from the stupidity of her friends.

Zander made a slight face and shrugged as they walked toward the dorms. "Technically speaking, I guess Elmhurst never actually said we were allowed to stay on the island during the weekend. What she did say was that we had to make sure we were in all of our classes during the week. There are no classes during the weekend, so we're not breaking those rules. She never mentioned anything about us having to sleep in our own beds every night, did she?"

"Nope. Not a word," Carson said with a wide grin. His exhaustion had vanished now that he was looking ahead to a weekend of camping at The Games. "She said we had permission to be in Scotland for the weekend so we could watch the Championships. I know I personally take that as meaning we can stay the night, as well."

"Are you sure about this?" Luna asked.

"Elmhurst didn't say we had to sleep at the academy," Vivi said. "And she said we could be in Scotland for the weekend."

"But you know she expects us to be in our rooms."

"Does she?" Zander asked.

He winked at Mia, and she blushed, looking away. "I think we should do it," she said. "It will be great to be there for the whole thing. And just think of how much research we're going to be able to do for our projects."

Luna finally relented. "All right. Let's pack."

They split up to get ready. They packed their clothes and toiletries quickly and met in front of the dorm building. Sleeping bags, blankets, lanterns, and cooking supplies, were piled at their feet. Mia didn't want anyone to see their gear. Although she had agreed to go and was excited about it, she had the nagging feeling in the back of her mind that they weren't supposed to be doing this.

It wasn't enough to stop her, though. She was too excited about going. The lure of Scotland was growing stronger, and she wanted to see what might be waiting for them there.

Their campsite was on the Isle of Skye, overlooking the Hebrides Sea. It was close to Glenbrittle, where the faerie pools were located. They dropped off their bags, and Mia turned to look at the ocean. The view was gorgeous, and she could see the Isle of Raasay, where they would go to watch The Games.

The two tents waiting for them were larger than Mia had expected and looked as comfortable as she could imagine tent-camping out here could be. But she braced for Vivi's evaluation of the sparse accommodations. There wasn't much by way of luxury going on, and while Mia thought of it as part of the experience, she didn't believe the Unseelie girl would be quite as understanding.

It seemed the others were expecting the same thing. Carson looked at her out of the corner of his eye as he unzipped the tent assigned to the boys, and tossed his bag inside, and Zander also watched her as he started building a rock circle for a fire pit.

But it turned out Vivi wasn't the one who complained about their situation. Instead, it was Luna. She stood back from the site and stared at the tents with distaste.

"What's wrong?" Mia asked.

"I just can't believe this is where we're staying for the whole weekend," Luna said.

"What's wrong with it?" Carson asked. "Look. The tents are even on platforms. We're going for the full pampering camping experience here."

"Yeah," Luna said. "The tents are fine, I guess. But I hate the thought of not having running water."

Carson scoffed. "We're not asking you to turn the woods into your own personal facilities, or to take a bath in the ocean, Luna. There are bathrooms with indoor plumbing, shower rooms, and everything."

Now it was time for Vivi to start voicing her opinion. "Shower rooms?" she said in disgust. "Ugh. I didn't think about us having to shower with other people. I really don't want to do that."

"You do it at school," Zander pointed out. "Why is it all right to do it there every day, but not here for a weekend?"

Vivi straightened and rolled her eyes at him as if she simply couldn't fathom why he didn't understand the issue. "That's not the same thing. There is a big difference between sharing a bathroom on a floor of halflings we know and go to school with, and showering in front of a bunch of women we've never even met."

Zander and Carson exchanged glances, unconvinced by the argument.

"Boys just don't get it," Luna said. "They probably would be perfectly fine with turning the woods into their own personal facilities and taking baths in the ocean."

Carson's words sounded more unpleasant coming out of her mouth. Zander sighed and looked at Mia. "You get it, don't you?" he asked.

Mia shrugged. "Sorry. I'm with the girls on this one. The tents are really nice, and I'm excited to be camping. But when it comes to showering with strangers, I'm siding with Vivi. But, I will say this is much better than having to trek back to the school every day."

The others nodded in agreement.

"Definitely," Zander said. "Especially since we aren't allowed to make our own portals anywhere on Earth. It would have been so much simpler if we could just get permission for you to make a portal to Scotland from your room. Then we could just go back and forth through it each day."

All five sighed, agreeing that would be so nice. Having their own personal portal would have made the travel so much easier, and they would get the benefit of being able to go whenever they wanted, and they wouldn't have to camp.

CHAPTER ELEVEN

Mia thought about the portals she had created when she hadn't meant to, well before she had fully understood what she was capable of. It had been such a shock at the time, and even now, she was still working on grasping the ability and creating portals reliably and effectively. This made her think of the others she created, and a blush came to her cheeks. She looked away to try to cover it, but Zander was watching her, and caught it.

"What is it, Mia?" he asked.

She sighed and shook her head. "It's really embarrassing."

"Tell us!" Vivi exclaimed. The others turned to stare at her, and she raised her shoulders. "What is camping for if not for sharing about ourselves and bonding?" she asked.

It was insincere, and so far out of Vivi's normal behavior that it was ludicrous, but they knew it was harmless and laughed.

"You don't have to tell us," Luna reassured her.

"But if you happen to have a good story and felt the need to divulge it, we wouldn't object," Carson said

Mia relented with a shake of her head and a smile. "All right. I'll tell you. I actually did make a portal over the summer."

"You're not supposed to do that," Luna pointed out. "Especially when you're not even on campus."

"I know. And after doing it, I think I probably know why. I figured since Elmhurst told us to do everything we could to practice our skills and strengthen our magic, it would be okay. Especially since I was with Cassia. She's a full fae and is trusted by Elmhurst. I thought it would be fine to get some practice in."

"Let me guess. It didn't go so well," Carson said.

"Not exactly. Well, not at first, anyway. The first couple of tries didn't go so great."

"You weren't able to make portals?" Vivi asked, clearly hoping Mia would admit she struggled. Somehow that would make it seem like Mia's strength and ability really did come from being on campus, or at least from being with the others.

"No. I was able to make them. That wasn't the problem. It was getting them to take me where I wanted to go that caused some issues," Mia said.

"Where did you end up?" Zander asked.

"In a creek," Mia admitted, hanging her head and covering her eyes. "One second, I was trying to send myself to the beach, and the next, I was on my back in a shallow creek. No injuries, thankfully." The other four giggled, and she smiled, feeling more relaxed now that she had admitted her struggles. "I don't know if that was better or worse than when I ended up in a cargo freighter."

"Did you see any pirates?" Carson asked.

They all stared at him, and his gaze flickered to each of them. "What? Pirates are cool."

They laughed, and Zander cocked his head a fraction. "What did you mean, that it didn't work out great *at first?*"

"Well, obviously, I was having a little bit of trouble to start with, but then I got hold of myself. I was able to create some that got me to just local places. Nothing too far away at first. Then I branched out some and was able to move a few states away at a time. But that was it. Nothing international worked for me."

"Where were you trying to go?" Vivi asked.

Mia didn't want to admit that she had been trying to return to Shanghai. She felt like she had unfinished business there and had wanted to see it again. "Just anywhere," she told Vivi.

"Well, if you were able to make all those portals during summer break, and Elmhurst didn't catch wind of it, you should be able to make some for us now," Carson said.

Mia shook her head. "No. Cassia was happy I was doing as well as I was. She agreed to talk to the headmistress about us being able to work together on making stronger, more effective portals during this semester, once the Narco situation is fully resolved. But until that happens, she agrees with Elmhurst. No portals. She gave me one stipulation. If there is mortal danger, and there's no other way out, I can try to make a portal. But that's a last-resort, a no-other-option thing."

"At least she's being reasonable." Vivi scoffed.

"Sort of. She went a little further. If I'm at school when it happens, I have to make a portal either to Elmhurst or to Cassia. I can't choose somewhere else," Mia added.

"What happens if both of them are in situations that put you in mortal danger too? Like, what if something happens to both Cassia and Elmhurst, and you're afraid for your life? It wouldn't make a whole lot of sense for you to portal yourself to the same place so you could be with them. And you shouldn't *not* get out of the danger because you wouldn't be headed to one of them. That seems a little counter-intuitive," Carson said.

"I don't think that was part of the planning," Mia said. "They probably figured if both of them were around me, I wasn't going to be in mortal danger. At least, that's what we're hoping."

"But it does still give you a loophole you could manipulate. What does serious danger mean, exactly? That could have all kinds of definitions," Carson pointed out.

"Absolutely not," Zander said. "We aren't going to have Mia make us a portal just because it would make things easier on us."

Carson made a face at him. "That's not what I meant. I'm just saying she probably shouldn't wait until the very second she feels like she is going to die and concentrate so much on making sure she gets to Elmhurst or Cassia."

"What do you mean?" Mia asked.

"No offense, Mia, but you aren't that great at making portals intentionally," Vivi said.

"I didn't hear you complaining about my portal-making skills when we were getting chased through the Louvre," Mia snapped. "They seemed to work out just fine for us then."

"Sort of. We traveled to different places in the museum, and still almost ended up getting killed. The point is, you can make a portal. I'll admit you are the only one of the five of us who can actually make one by yourself. But you're not great at doing it reliably, or at getting to a place you want to be."

"The five of us can do it together," Mia suggested. "If something dangerous happened and we needed to get away, we could combine our powers and make one to get us away to somewhere safer."

"With all of us concentrating on it, we could do it," Luna said.

"But it takes too long," Carson said. "Don't you remember how long it actually takes to make a usable portal when we merge our powers? If we're in danger, we're not going to want to stand around trying to achieve the Power of Five so we can portal our way to Elmhurst."

"Did you just argue against yourself?" Mia asked.

Carson paused. "I don't know."

"I think the point is if something happens and Mia is in serious danger, getting her out of the situation as fast as possible is going to be the top priority. She's proven her ability to use portals to get her out of danger when it's needed. But it's not something to play with," Zander said. "We don't want to try to use it just because she gets spooked, or wants a shower without thirty other people in the same room with her."

"So, we're in agreement," Mia said. "Portals are a last resort."

They all nodded, but she felt a heaviness hanging over them. She didn't want them thinking about the danger and the fear. She didn't want to think about Narco and all he had planned for her. They were in Scotland to have fun and to experience new things.

"Come on." Zander seemed to sense her discomfort. "Let's go to the faerie pools."

A short walk took them to the path that led to the pools. Mia was immediately in awe of the beauty surrounding her. The path wove gently into the distance, taking them through peat bogs and towering rocks. Waterfalls tumbled down some of the stones, sparkling in the sunlight and forming little pools in the crevices. It was all so beautiful, so mesmerizing, Mia almost wanted to stop and enjoy it. But every time she slowed down, Zander would gently pull on her hand, or Luna would laugh and coax her forward.

"Come on!" Luna said. "There's so much more."

"It's so amazing here," Mia said. "How could it be better?"

Zander tugged on her fingertips again. "Let's get to the actual pools and find out."

CHAPTER TWELVE

Something fluttered by at the edge of Mia's vision. It got her attention, and she tried to find it again, to no avail. It wasn't an insect or a bird, but something bright, small, and fluttery had zipped past her arm and disappeared into the woods just off the path. She strained her eyes to see, but it was either long gone or standing still, camouflaged by the trees, leaves, and tall grass.

"Mia?" Luna asked, stopping beside her on the path to scan her face with concern, trying to read her.

Mia shook her head and smiled, turning her attention away from the deep woods. "Hmm?"

"You were saying something," Luna said, still studying her face. She was looking at the spot Mia had been staring at. "Then you just stopped talking and started staring over there. Did you see something?"

"I don't think so," she said, and then something moved, zipping across the sky and down on the other side of the path. "Look!" she exclaimed, pointing.

The others, who were ahead of them, suddenly stopped in their tracks and tried to see what Mia was pointing at. Zander ran back to them, followed by Carson and Vivi, with Cinder zipping along over Carson's shoulder.

"Is that a faerie?" Vivi asked.

Ignoring her, Mia walked off the path toward the now stationary sprite, hovering above a patch of long weeds that covered the embankment of one of the pools.

"Hi there," she said, trying to sound as non-threatening as possible. "I'm a friend. Can you talk to us?"

The faerie, seemingly spooked, shot up in the air and dove again, corkscrewing into the pool and out of sight. Mia stared at the water for a moment and saw another faerie, or at least she assumed it was a different one, zipping out of the pool and flying off into the woods. No water came up with them. Not even a ripple in the stillness of the pool.

"I wonder if the pools are portals," said Mia, climbing back up onto the path,

"Duh, of course, they are," said Cinder, incredulously. "How do you think the faeries get from Faerie to Earth so fast all the time?"

There was a temporary silence as everyone turned to Cinder, and the attention made her cheeks flush. She folded her arms. "What?" Cinder exclaimed.

"Hold up one second…" Carson began to speak.

Mia took over when Carson failed to follow it up in his shock. "You mean to tell me that these faeries don't actually live on Earth? That they travel through these portals back and forth to where they live, in freaking Faerie?"

Now the red-faced Cinder turned her nose in the air and crossed her legs as her wings beat rapidly, keeping her floating in a position that made it look like she was sitting. "You really didn't know?" she asked huffily. "All this time you have known me, and all this studying you do, and you didn't know?"

"No, I did not," said Mia evenly.

"Neither did I." Zander backed her up.

"Even *I* didn't know that," muttered Luna.

"We all thought the fae who guarded the pools lived here and didn't go to Faerie," Vivi said.

Cinder looked at each of them, her tiny hand over her chest now, as if she was shocked. Then the shock turned to frustrated anger, and she gritted her teeth as she floated around them. Her voice, which was barely intelligible at the best of times, became a squeaking, high-pitched wall of noise as she dive-bombed between them, undoubtedly yelling at them all. But the more worked up she got, offended to the highest degree at their ignorance, she began to sneeze. Dust flew from her as she did so, and before long, the halflings' feet were leaving the ground.

"Uh, Cinder?" Carson called the pixie.

"Shh, let her figure it out," Vivi interrupted, and lay back, allowing the magic to float her in the air. "Just enjoy it."

"Hey, look at me. I'm Superman!" Zander shouted.

He was higher than the rest, faerie dust covering his hair where he had been the target of a direct sneeze. He was locked in a pose with one arm outstretched, hand balled in a fist, and his other cocked by his side. His legs were straight out, and he looked as though he was flying across the sky in one powerful motion.

"Yeah, well, I'm Peter Pan!" yelled Carson, suddenly getting into the spirit. "Thanks, Tink!" he shouted at Cinder, which only served to make her screeching even worse.

Luna and Mia floated lower than the others, having not been subjected to direct blasts of the pixie's dust. Still, it was enough to break the tension of the moment, and soon laughter filled the air and began to attract attention. Faeries began to close ranks around the pools, guarding them from the laughing, floating halflings wandering near them. They hadn't trusted them before, and now they had more reason not to.

Cinder, having yelled until her throat was hoarse, slowed down and slumped into a large open flower. She lay back for a moment before sitting up and waggling a finger at Carson one last time. She fell back again, exhausted. The group continued to enjoy the floating until the magic began to wear off, and when they all were on solid ground again, Zander went to Cinder and offered his hand.

"We're sorry, Cinder. Would you like to join us now?" he said.

Reluctantly, Cinder hopped into his hand, and he picked her up and placed her on his shoulder. This bit of respect seemed to appease her, and everyone returned to the path. Before long, faeries were popping up from the little pools and following them. Some hung back far away, watching with suspicious eyes, while others floated out of arm's reach.

As they neared the area outside the main pools, Vivi tugged at Mia's elbow. "Look, there's one of them over there behind that scrub brush between us and the stream. See it?"

"I do," Mia said.

"I'm going to try to catch it," Vivi said. "Watch."

"No, Vivi. I really don't think that's a good ide—" Mia was too late.

Vivi was already halfway down the path and almost at the spot where she had seen a faerie hiding. As she reached out to touch it, the faerie panicked, and a blast of dust filled the air. Unlike Cinder's dust, which either set something on fire or made things float, this was more explosive in nature. Vivi was flung backward fifteen feet and landed with a sound, not unlike a hammer being slammed into a custard pie.

Cinder began to laugh uproariously as everyone rushed to Vivi. She had been blown directly into a mud puddle in a bog and was now covered from head to toe in slick, brown goop. She was frantically trying to wipe it away with hands also covered in the stuff, which only served to remove some mud and replace it with more. A rather impressive series of expletives streamed from her mouth as she struggled to gain her footing, slipped, and fell back again.

"Will someone please help me?" she shouted, sitting there dejectedly.

Cinder was now laughing so hard, she was snorting, causing tiny bits of flame to shoot from her nose and land on dry leaves on the path. Tiny brush fires began to spring up, and within seconds, the group was shut off from returning to the path by a wall of yellow flame.

A sound like a hummingbird rattled and buzzed near Mia's ear as a faerie zipped by, casting some of her own dust on the flames and putting them out. A harsh, but unintelligible conversation was held between Cinder and the heroic faerie before it zipped along to Vivi in the mud while everyone else moved back onto the path.

"What did she say?" Carson whispered to Cinder.

"She scolded me for being careless," muttered Cinder, embarrassed.

The faerie helped Vivi out of the bog and back onto the path, and with a quick pass around her head, a spray of glittering dust fell on the girl that dissolved the mud in seconds. In the span of a few breaths, Vivi's clothes were dry, and only the faintest hint of her mud-scapade was visible underneath her fingernails.

"Thank you so much," Vivi said gratefully. "I really appreciate it, thank you."

It struck Mia how nice Vivi was being to the faerie. Sure, the faerie had just saved her more embarrassment, but still, Vivi being that nice to anyone was not to be expected. It was a remarkable transformation, and Mia wondered if, while Vivi may not be a friend yet, she could at least count on her now to be an ally, and the effect on her had been positive. Who knew, maybe by the end of the school year Vivi *could* be a friend after all.

CHAPTER THIRTEEN

The hike continued, and for the most part, the group was in high spirits. All except for Cinder, that is. Most of the time, she sat on Mia's shoulder, sulking, and when she didn't have her fist shoved into her cheek, elbow resting on her thigh, she was sighing heavily and crossing her arms over her chest.

Mia resisted the urge to talk to her and try to cheer her up. It would only result in more huffing and puffing, and possibly a rant. Not wanting her hair on fire, Mia opted for silence— better safe than sorry.

Still, Mia wanted to find a way to get the pixie out of her funk, and as the group walked closer to a large pool, Mia pushed ahead of them. When she reached the very edge of the water, she looked down, seeing her face reflected in the shimmering pale blue water. She watched Cinder's reflection as the faerie took in her own image and smiled a little. Mia suspected no matter how down Cinder was, she couldn't be depressed around these pools.

"Cinder?" said someone from nearby. Both Mia and Cinder spun toward the voice.

Cinder jumped up and stood on Mia's shoulders. She knew that voice, but it had been a while since she had heard it. "Alania?"

Cinder exclaimed and took off from Mia's shoulders, diving toward the sound.

A bright purplish light rose from the high grass, and when she squinted, Mia could just make out the shape of another faerie. Cinder tackled her in mid-air, and they tumbled backward in an embrace, laughter filling the area and drawing the attention of the rest of the halflings, who were quickly approaching.

"What's going on?" Vivi asked.

"Beats me," Mia responded.

The two faeries shot back up into the air, chattering away at a speed and pitch that made it impossible for the halflings to understand. They stood in a slightly uncomfortable silence until Cinder realized she hadn't introduced them yet. Gliding down on gossamer wings, Cinder and Alania hovered between Mia and the crew.

"Everybody, this is Alania, my cousin!" Cinder exclaimed and wrapped her arms around Alania's neck in a tight hug.

"Shh, Cinder, you need to calm down. I am excited to see you too, but you know how the elders get," Alania responded.

"How do the elders get?" Zander asked, suddenly on the defensive.

"Oh, you're fine," Cinder said. "It's me they would be mad at. They would ask me to leave."

"Again," Alania added.

"Yes, again," grumbled Cinder. "Anyway, this is my cousin, and she's the best."

"We spent the first thirty years of our lives growing up together in Faerie. I got chosen to be a guardian in training and Cinder…" Alania's voice trailed away.

"I was punished for not having enough control of my powers and was sent to Elmhurst. So now you know the story, and if you say anything to anyone, I will light your nose-hairs on fire."

"That is an oddly specific, and wholly frightening threat," Carson said.

"There's a reason for that," Alania said.

The group waited for her to elaborate, but nothing followed, so Mia decided to move on. "Why Elmhurst?" Mia asked.

"Cinder has a knack, if you will, for cleaning. Her magic is especially suited to keeping things tidy, and they need all the help they can get in buildings filled with teenagers," Alania explained. "So, she was sent there as a favor to them, and as a sort of punishment for her."

"It worked out. I enjoy being there, and I got to meet you guys," Cinder said.

"Well, it's good to meet you, Alania. Any family of Cinder's is a friend to us," Zander said. "My name is Zander, and this is Carson, Vivi, Luna, and Mia."

Alania's eyes lingered a little longer on Mia, and it wasn't lost on her. It was as if the faerie saw something she didn't quite believe. She kept a close eye on Mia as she poked her cousin with her elbow and whispered to her.

"Hmm?" Cinder asked her as they glided back a few feet.

"Who is this Mia?" Alania asked in hushed tones.

"Oh, well, that's an interesting story," Cinder said, a bit louder than Alania had hoped for, and just loud enough for Mia to catch some of it. "It's a big secret. I'll tell you when nobody else is around."

Mia was about to ask Cinder what she had said and why she was being so secretive, but she was interrupted.

"Maybe you could help us," Luna said, getting the faerie's attention. "We are doing a class project on Scottish Fae lore. The faerie pools would make a really neat subject to do the paper on, and someone of your knowledge could really help get us the most comprehensive and accurate information about this wonderful place. I know as far as grades go, that would be an A for sure."

"Luna, do you have any idea how many students are going to be doing a paper on the pools?" Carson asked. "Like, everybody.

All of the students are allowed to visit, which means *all of the students are going to visit*. They are all going to have the same idea. Even if none of them get the inside scoop from a real faerie, it's going to still end up being one of a million reports on the pools. We might bore our teacher to death."

"He has a point there," Vivi said. "We should try to find some other topic to write about."

A series of nods was enough to convince Luna. "Okay, fine. If not the pools, what else then?"

"Well," said Mia, after a moment or two of contemplative silence. "I would like to learn more about Princess Caledona."

At the mention of the princess, Alania's gaze snapped to Mia, and her jaw dropped. Mia didn't see it, but Cinder did, and she lifted her finger to shut her cousin's mouth. "What do you know about Princess Caledona?" Alania stammered at last, pushing Cinder's finger away.

"Not a whole lot, really. We found an ancient text in the school's library. One we thought was supposed to be in the restricted area, but it was out in plain sight. It was old, like really old, and seemed to be the writing of a historian from just after the time that the Romans conquered Scotland. It had one story about her in it, more of a small biography really. Just that she lived, was really powerful, and she helped the Picts, and that after she died, they were beaten back, and their land was conquered."

"Stolen," Alania muttered under her breath.

"What was that?" Vivi asked.

"Nothing. Go on."

"Well, that's it, really. There wasn't much else in the story, and we had never heard of her before then," Mia responded. "Is there something you know? It would really help us out for our project, and honestly, I'm just really intrigued."

For the first time since they had met the faerie, Alania was silent. It was odd, but the rest of the group was already deep in conversation, talking about how they would stretch out the story if they needed too, and who would be tasked with doing all the legwork to research the Roman Expansion. Which left Mia, Cinder, and Alania standing quietly together.

After a few moments, Cinder seemed to think of something. "So, how's the guardian thing going?"

"Great," Alania replied.

"Great? Just great? Nothing else?"

"What do you expect?" Alania said. "No one comes here except faerie. Until now, of course. I had yet to see any students before your friends showed up, but I've heard that others were filtering in and out. The boy is right though, most of them are trying to learn as much as possible about the pools. They all miss the magic stored in the forest trees. All they ever think of is the water."

"What about the trees?" Mia asked.

"The trees are of the Earth. They are concentrated with thousands of years of magic. The water just transfers energy, lets us make portals, and can be used for protection. But the trees are where the real magic lies. Without the trees, the pools become just simple water. The Picts knew that."

"Did Princess Caledona teach them?" Mia asked. Alania's lips pursed in a tight smile, and another moment of awkward silence followed.

Cinder patted Mia on the head in a way the little faerie probably intended as reassurance, but made the halfling feel like a puppy instead. Mia glared at her, but Cinder simply smiled.

"Don't worry about the princess," she said. "You have plenty of time. You'll find out more about the ancient girl, I promise."

Mia decided to let go of her frustration. "Do you think there's enough information out there for me to do a paper on Princess Caledona?" she asked.

Cinder nodded enthusiastically. "Definitely. You'll be able to find everything you need to write an amazing paper."

To the side, Alania's eyes widened, and one little hand slapped over her mouth to stop her from saying anything. She mumbled for a few seconds as if her voice was doing everything it could to push past her hand and get something out, but she was fighting to hold it back.

Cinder glanced at her, then looked back at Mia and smiled as she grabbed hold of Alania. She pulled her cousin back and dragged her away to a spot far enough from the group that they wouldn't be heard talking. Her gaze flickered back to the group, and she was relieved to see Mia already falling into a conversation with Luna rather than watching her.

"Be quiet!" she hissed at Alania.

"I didn't say anything," her cousin said.

"And you're not going to say anything. You can't. Nothing. Not a single word and not to anyone. Understand? Mia's life is already in danger," Cinder insisted.

"I'm not going to say anything," Alania agreed. "I won't tell anyone. And the faerie guardians will help protect her if Mia asks."

Cinder gave a slight sigh of relief. "Thank you. I appreciate your help."

CHAPTER FOURTEEN

The voice was almost like the shadows themselves. Narco watched the darkness around him shifting and morphing, moving with the wind and the will of the shadowy space around the trees. The branches reached out and clawed at each other, scraping and tangling as they moved and swayed with the rush of the air.

Fog swirled around them. It wove between the trees, climbing up higher into the top branches before sinking low where it crawled and slunk across the ground. It seemed to breathe, and if he listened closely, Narco could almost hear it whispering, but there were no words. It drew closer to him, pressing against his skin as though the forest drew in a breath. An instant later, it sank away again and dissipated into the trees.

The man in front of Narco moved slightly to one side, shifting his weight from one leg to the other. The shadows appeared to move with him. They combined with the shade cast from his hat to conceal his face. Narco couldn't see him fully, but it didn't matter. He knew who the man was, and he didn't need the confirmation of his eyes.

"What are you saying?" Narco growled.

"I can't just kill the girl without confirmation of her being a descendant of Princess Violet. Too many fae know about her. She is being talked about in circles all throughout Faerie," the man said.

"What do you mean she is being talked about?" Narco demanded.

"Some are curious about her abilities. They saw the video you posted and can't help but notice the types of things she was able to do. Things most halflings shouldn't be able to do at her point in their training. People are wondering about her," the man said.

"It will be fine," Narco replied. "It was only a video. There have been many more showing many other things."

"It wasn't just a video," the man snapped. "She is becoming too well-known. You should never have put that video up. Thank Faerie Elmhurst had it pulled down within just a few hours of it going up, but too many fae saw it. The reaction is spreading, and it isn't good. Some fae who saw it have stretched the truth on what she did, and people are believing them. Others are saying it was a hoax and don't think any of it really happened. But that doesn't matter. So many are gossiping about her, it's created a damaging situation. Your idiotic decision has made everything much more complicated. She can't just disappear or die. Not without good reason. Too many know of her and have questions about her abilities. They will notice, and it will come back."

"Then we have to make sure no one thinks anything strange. It can be done," Narco insisted.

"Remember, Narco, this is my assignment. You work for me. I control your destiny. Your future, or lack thereof, is in my hands. You don't want to disappoint me. With all you have done, and all the fae you have crossed, few would wonder what happened should something befall you," the man threatened.

His voice had lowered to an ominous, gravelly growl.

"It will all work out. It will be exactly as it is meant to be," Narco reassured him, almost stumbling over himself to try to appease the shadow man. "People can talk, but unless they have proof, they will soon forget what they thought they saw, or what it could mean. It will mean nothing when she's gone. People talk and make things up and try to find meaning in everything. There will be something else that comes along to distract them, and they won't give her another thought. So, when it is time for her to be eliminated, it won't be of any concern to any of them."

"I can only hope you're right," the shadow man said. "If you're not, there will be consequences."

"I understand," Narco said.

"And speaking of proof, I will need it from you. This is something that can't be taken lightly. It can't be guessed or estimated. I need you to bring me physical, irrefutable proof that this girl is a direct descendant of the royal line. I must have absolute proof that cannot be argued. Only then will I know for sure this girl is the one I have been looking for. Without that proof, I won't accept her. Do you understand?" the man asked.

"Yes. I understand," Narco told him. "I will get you proof. You will know she's the one. I'm sure of it."

The shadow man gave a slow nod, almost imperceptible within the movement of the darkness and fog around him. Narco only knew he was making the gesture by the slight tip of the dark edge of the hat toward him.

The nod wasn't fully a sign of confidence, or a show that the man believed in Narco and his assertions. It didn't mean he trusted Narco or thought he would come through and do what was expected of him. But it was an acknowledgment. It said he had heard what Narco had told him and was willing to at least give him the time and the opportunity to make it happen. It was all Narco could cling to for now.

Without another word, the man turned and walked away from him. Narco stayed in place, watching him as he disappeared into the trees and the shadows beyond. It almost looked as if the fog was reaching to take hold of him, pulling him in so the rest of the forest could swallow him whole. But Narco knew that couldn't be. The forest wouldn't want him.

"Proof," he muttered to himself when the man was out of sight. "He wants me to bring him physical proof. What does that even mean?"

He thought about it for a few seconds. His assignment was to bring the descendant of Princess Violet to his boss so she could be dealt with once and for all. But with all the mistakes and missteps along the way, the man had lost his confidence in Narco. He no longer trusted in Narco's skill or his reputation. He needed absolute proof that would ensure they had the right girl this time.

"The only thing that would truly prove lineage would be DNA. But would that really do anything? Do they have DNA on file for the last king and queen?" He considered his options for a moment. Maybe he could compare Mia's DNA to that of the Unseelie Queen?

He continued whispering to himself, trying to determine if going after Mia's DNA would have any real benefit. It would be definitive proof of her being a member of the royal family, but it wouldn't do any good if they didn't have any proven royal DNA to compare it to.

He thought about it for a few more minutes and didn't come up with any other idea for the type of proof the shadow man wanted. He wasn't exactly sure it was going to work, but it was all he could think of at the moment. He was going to get Mia's DNA.

All he had to do was come up with how he was going to get it. His mind drifted to that shock of strange red hair that set her so boldly apart from the other halflings. A few strands of that from her brush would be enough.

CHAPTER FIFTEEN

The walk along the path seemed to stretch out the longer they were on it. Mia wondered if that was the same type of effect as the classes on Fridays but in reverse. Their campsite didn't seem like it was far away from the faerie pools, but she was so excited to get to them and see what the fuss was all about, it seemed it took longer the closer they got. At least she had the fun of talking with her friends and looking at the lush surroundings as she went.

But finally, the path took a sharper slant upward, and they emerged from the tighter, peat-lined path to the open space of the pools. It was nothing short of breathtaking. Mia had seen beautiful things, and been amazed by the world around her before, but nothing like this.

Everything she had ever experienced, all she had ever seen, paled in comparison to the faerie pools. An array of pink, blue, and purple hues, filled the air, creating a shimmering mist around the large pools. Little waterfalls glinted in the sunlight and danced with reflections of the colors as they came down the side of the mountain, and poured into the pools. The sound around them was almost as entrancing as the sight. The water trickled along the rocks and bubbled into the pools, blending with the laughter of all the faeries playing among them.

They were everywhere. All around the water, perched on the rocks, flitting in the air, splashing in the pools, hundreds of little faeries with big eyes and swishing wings played. Some rode the waterfalls like slides, and others swirled in the spray that came off them. They giggled and whispered, all turning to watch the halflings as they came to the pools. Most of those big, wide eyes were focused directly on Mia. She felt like they knew something about her, almost as though they expected her to be there. And at the same time, there was an uncertainty about it, as if they weren't sure about her.

One flew up to them and bowed her head to Mia. The halfling was stunned by the little creature's appearance. Like with all faeries, she was beautiful, with a creamy complexion, and shimmery silver wings. But it wasn't her beauty that immediately caught Mia's attention. Instead, it was her hair. Flaming red, it tumbled down her shoulders and along her back. A bold reminder of Scotland, but also of Mia's own differences that made her stand out against the other halfling fae.

"Welcome, Mia and friends."

The greeting took Mia aback and she looked at the others around her. They stared back, as surprised as she was.

"Hello," Mia said. "How do you know my name?"

"I am Guardian Myla. I am the Head Guardian of the Faeries. It has been my responsibility, my duty, and my privilege, to guard the Faerie Pools against intruders for the last three thousand years."

"Three thousand years?" Mia asked, astonished by the incredible length of time.

"Yes. I became the head guardian just as the Romans invaded Caledonia."

Mia looked at Zander.

"Caledonia is the former name of Scotland," he whispered.

As soon as he said it, Mia remembered reading that in one of the books she was using for research. It was a brief mention, so short and inconsequential it hadn't even stuck with her as they continued their investigation. But now the memory made her think of something else.

"Was Princess Caledona named for the land?" she asked.

For several long seconds, the head guardian stared back at Mia. Mia felt scrutinized, as if in that stare, she was suddenly the only person who existed, and no one else mattered. The intentional focus in the faerie's eyes was almost too much, and Mia couldn't fathom what she might be thinking. Perhaps Mia had asked the wrong thing or brought up something she shouldn't have. But a huge grin broke out across Myla's lovely face, and she nodded happily.

"Yes," she said. "Yes, the land's first princess was named for the region. Princess Caledona. That's right. And now, welcome." She gestured to the water all around them. "Welcome to the faerie pools. I'm sure you have heard many stories about the amazing properties of the water. I cannot promise that what you have heard is true. I also cannot promise you that it is not. You are welcome to come closer and enjoy the waters. But be careful."

Her voice suddenly became more serious and intense. The five halflings had started walking toward the water but paused and looked at the head guardian.

"Be careful of what?" Zander asked.

"You must stay clear of certain pools. You cannot get anywhere near them, and should not touch the water. You shouldn't even let the spray from them touch your skin. The water is very powerful, and can be very dangerous to halflings," Myla cautioned them.

"Which pools?" Mia asked. "How will we know if we are getting near water that will hurt us?"

She wanted the guardian faerie to give them specific instructions, to point out the areas of the waters that weren't safe, but

Myla didn't. Instead, she looked Mia directly in the eyes for another intense second, then glanced back at the faeries still playing in and around the pools.

"The faeries will tell you. Just pay attention to them, and they will let you know if you are getting too close to any of the dangerous areas."

"I'll keep an eye out for you, too," Carson said. "And make sure you're paying attention to what the faeries say."

"You're not getting in the water?" Vivi asked.

Carson shook his head. "No. I'm fine out here."

Zander eyed the water, his face uncertain. Mia moved closer to him. "Are you going to get in?" she asked hopefully.

"I want to," he acknowledged. "But I'm not sure about the cold."

"Oh, don't worry about that," Alania said, suddenly making herself known again after insisting on staying silent for the rest of the walk after her confrontation with Cinder. "The water is warm for those of fae descent. Even halflings. You should get in and enjoy it."

Luna and Vivi exchanged glances. Neither of them had made a move to get into the water. Mia suspected they were thinking about the halflings they had overheard talking in the stands at the slamball game, and the conflicting opinions they had all had on the effects of the water.

"What does the water do?" she asked. "Can it hurt us?"

"What do you mean?" Myla asked.

"We've heard a lot of things. Some people have told us the water can harm humans and even fae. You said that there are some pools that are dangerous to halflings, but are the other ones safe for us?" Vivi asked.

Around the halflings, the air filled with the tinkling, musical sound of hundreds of little faeries laughing at the question. One particularly young-looking faerie who was sitting on a rock laughed so hard she wrapped her arms around her stomach and toppled backward into the pool behind her. A spray of water came up after her, colored in hues of pink and purple, and filled with tiny specks of glitter.

"Those must have been some stories," Myla said. Then she smiled and gave them a conspiratorial, almost mischievous look. "Don't let it worry you. The faeries like to come up with those stories and spread them around for people to hear. We have to come up with some scary myths about the place, or too many fae would come in search of the mythic Water of Life."

That had all the halflings perking up. They looked at each other, their eyebrows raised as they silently asked each other if they knew what she was talking about.

When none of them volunteered any information to each other, Zander turned to Myla. "What is the Water of Life?"

The head guardian waved her graceful little hand dismissively.

"It's nothing. Only a myth. There is no true Water of Life. But it stems from the story of Princess Caledona, the first princess of the land Mia asked about. She was well-known and beloved in this region. She was unusual and alluring to all who knew her or even knew *of* her. There were many things about her that were truly amazing. Because she had so many powers and lived for hundreds of years, many people assumed she had found some way of extending her life. They thought perhaps she had been the one to discover the fountain of youth. But, alas, it didn't exist. There isn't any water source around here that will extend the life of a human. Not even one so wonderful as the Princess."

CHAPTER SIXTEEN

The five halflings sagged, all a little deflated by the declaration from the head guardian.

"Well, that burst my bubble a little," Luna said. "It would have been fun to find out there really is a Fountain of Youth."

"You're still teenagers," Cinder pointed out. "Maybe you shouldn't start worrying about trying to figure out ways not to get older. At least, not yet."

The halflings laughed, and the girls again considered entering the water. But as soon as Luna and Vivi walked toward the nearest pool, Carson took several steps back. Mia saw the movement and the look of worry on his face. This was not like Carson at all. She had expected him to be the most enthusiastic about getting into the pools. In fact, she had been preparing herself to deal with him being ridiculous, to try to ride some of the waterfalls the way the faeries were.

She inched over to him. "What's wrong?" He shook his head, but she wasn't dissuaded. "Come on. Let's get in. I actually thought you were going to be the most troublesome of all of us. I figured it was a distinct possibility you were going to get yourself hurt messing around here, and we were going to have to explain it to Elmhurst."

"Thanks for your vote of confidence," Carson said flatly.

"What is it? What's wrong?" He shook his head again, easing farther away from the water. "You've been here before, haven't you?"

This time, Carson reacted. His eyes got slightly wider, and he gulped heavily. "As a small child."

Beside them, Myla suddenly laughed. She nodded. "Ah, yes. The boy who fell in." She laughed again, but Carson didn't seem to see any of the humor in the situation.

"What is that all about?" Zander asked. "What does she mean the boy who fell in?"

Carson didn't say anything, so Myla smiled at the group. "I thought I recognized Carson when I first saw him. Of course, it has been many years since I last saw him, and he has changed very much. But I will never forget when he was last here. He was a very small boy when he came here with his human family. The water has little meaning to humans, with the exception of some areas, but it is different for the halflings. Because Carson is a halfling, he was able to get close enough to the pools to find a portal. It fascinated him, of course, and he wanted to play. Before anyone was able to warn him or help him, he toppled off the rocks and into the water. The portal immediately took control of him and sent him to another place."

"Where did you go?" Mia asked Carson, but he shrugged and shook his head.

"I don't know," he said. "I know it was a portal and it took me somewhere, but I have no idea where. No one was able to tell me. I was terrified."

"One of the guardians was able to rescue him and bring him back. When he did, Carson told everyone wherever he had gone was full of monsters. Of course, none of them knew what he was talking about, and they figured he was just a frightened little boy trying to understand something he had never experienced before. But he was insistent. He described what he saw wherever the portal took him as monsters. His family took him and left," Myla said.

"And we never came back here," Carson said. "Can you blame me? They were monsters. At least, that's what they seemed like to me at the time. I don't know what they really were, but to my mind, when I was that little, they were monsters. It was the only way I could think of to describe them. They were absolutely horrible, and I was scared out of my mind. I think it might have scared my family even more. They knew what I was, of course, and that I was going to be different. I already knew of magic and had started playing with some silly little spells. But they didn't know what to think or do when that happened. It was the first time the fae half of me put me into a type of danger they weren't able to see or fend off for me."

"Do you think you went to Faerie?" Mia asked.

Myla's face became more serious, and she looked at the halflings pointedly. "There are portals here that go to very dangerous places. That is why we are here. It's not just to keep the visiting fae and humans from damaging the pools, or hurting themselves. They must be protected from the portals. We are here to guard the links. No one should go through them. Not ever. Those portals aren't safe for anyone and must be avoided. Carson was very fortunate that he was very young, and the guardians were watching him closely. The instant he fell, a guardian was already after him and was able to bring him back very quickly. He likely feels he was there for a long time, and it probably felt that way because of how frightening it was for him. But Carson was safe. He was brought back quickly, and couldn't be hurt. Others who have gone through were not that lucky."

She didn't expressly say Carson falling into the pool when he was young had sent him into a portal to Faerie, but all the halflings assumed that's what she meant. There were several seconds of tension before Carson took another step backward.

Mia knew it was best to let him be. Myla had started telling the story of his childhood visit as if it was a very funny event, but it had ended far more ominously. Carson wasn't going to go near the water, and Mia couldn't blame him. He was courageous enough to have come this far. He would be fine to sit on the rocks and watch his friends have fun.

Which was exactly what Zander wanted to do. He wasn't wasting any more time. He removed shoes and stepped into the water. He was cautious at first, not knowing how much he trusted Myla's assurance that the pools were warm. But when his toes touched the water, it was soothing, almost like bath-water. He sank the rest of his foot in and walked into the pool. The warmth enveloped him, and he sank down to his shoulders.

"Come on," he invited Mia. "It feels good."

She shook her head. "Not right now."

The story of the portal had been enough to take away her desire to enter the pools, at least for now, but she was enjoying watching Zander. Beside her, Luna appeared to have forgotten they were on a trip for the weekend and was back in school mode.

"What can you tell me about the history of the pools?" she asked a faerie who had come to settle on the rock beside Luna. "Did they always look like this? Have they changed much in the last three thousand years?"

"I thought we were here to enjoy the pools and have fun," Vivi pointed out.

"We agreed to stay for the weekend because it would give us so much time to explore and do research for our projects," Luna retorted.

Mia laughed. "Leave it to you to be very literal with that conversation."

"Covering all her bases," Zander said from the water.

"You'll all be jealous when we get back to school, and *I* have all the research," Luna teased. She turned her attention back to the faerie. "What about the rest of the area? What's the history of the island, and that area where we're camping? Did people used to live there?"

Mia chuckled and turned to watch Zander. He slid through the water slowly, appearing to revel in the feeling of it on his skin. Carson and Vivi were off somewhere together, and Mia continued to listen to Luna, and watch Zander for the next hour.

Suddenly, she sensed eyes on the back of her head. It felt like she was being watched. She assumed it was the faeries who had been fascinated by her since they had first arrived. They had been paying her a great deal of attention since the five had walked up to the pools. After a few seconds, she acknowledged it felt different. She wasn't just registering the little creatures' curiosity about her. The feeling was making the hair on her arms and the back of her neck stand on end.

It was a very strange sensation, different from the slight discomfort of having so many faeries watching her at once. She hated it. As much as she had wanted to see the pools when they had first arrived in Scotland, now all she wanted was to get away from them.

CHAPTER SEVENTEEN

"Hey, guys," Mia said. "I think maybe we should start heading back. It's getting dark."

Vivi and Carson appeared at her side. They had been walking around the pools, looking into the water, and talking with some of the faeries.

Luna stopped grilling the faerie sitting beside her, and looked around. "Wow. You're right. I didn't realize it was already getting so late," she said. "We should head back to our tents and get ready for bed."

"Yeah. We're getting up early for the games," Zander reminded them. "I forgot we already went to school all day today."

He climbed out of the pool and looked down at his soaked clothes. He shivered, suddenly cold now that he wasn't in the soothing heated water of the pool. One of the little faeries rushed up to him, and in a shower of sparkles, dried him off.

He smiled at her. "Thank you. That would have made for an unpleasant walk back to the campground."

"Speaking of which," Vivi said. "It's really dark. Did everybody bring a flashlight with them?"

Mia picked up her backpack, which was sitting at her feet,

and unzipped it. She dug through the few things inside and found her flashlight at the bottom. She flipped it on and held it up for the others to see. "I've got mine," she said.

Zander checked up his bag and retrieved his own light. "I have mine, too," he announced.

Carson, Vivi, and Luna followed suit, and soon all five beams of light were shining up into the sky. As bright as the flashlights had seemed while they had still been surrounded by the colorful glows of the pools, it was quickly apparent they wouldn't be nearly as beneficial once they got onto the path leading back to the campsite.

"It won't be so long a walk this time," Myla reassured them. "When it gets dark, there is a small bus that comes to the bottom of this path to take visitors up the path to the campsites. It helps to keep visitors safe, and also prevents them from trying to remain here at the pools overnight."

"People aren't allowed at the pools at night?" Luna asked.

"It would not be safe." Myla didn't elaborate.

Several of the faeries gathered around them, and one fluttered closer. "We would be happy to guide you down the path," she offered.

"I will be with them as well," Cinder said.

Mia glanced at the pixie, realizing she had forgotten Cinder and her cousin Alania were there with them. They had been so quiet during the visit that they melded in with the rest of the faeries.

Myla smiled. "Thank you. Take them down and wait with them until the bus comes." She turned her attention to Mia again. "You are all welcome to visit again."

"Thank you," Mia said. "Perhaps we will."

With the faeries around them and the beams of their flash-lights shining on the ground, the halflings walked back down the peat-lined path to the bus pickup point. Several yards along the path, Vivi gave the others a deliberate look. Her expression drew them closer so she could whisper without the faeries listening in.

"Did everyone else feel eyes on the backs of your heads while we were leaving?" she asked.

"I did," Mia admitted.

The others nodded, murmuring their own confirmations.

"It was really freaky," Carson said. "It was like someone was watching us. Someone other than the faeries."

Though the walk hadn't been very long to reach the pools in the first place, Mia found herself grateful for the idea of a ride back to the tents. She was tired and looked forward to settling in for the night. But, the way her mind was churning, she could only hope she would be able to relax.

Mia was relieved, almost two hours later, when they were changed, and tucked into their sleeping bags in the tent. She tried to push away the sensations of being watched, and the strange feelings of the pools, and concentrate on the next day. She was looking forward to seeing more of the sights of the Isle of Skye, and to go to the Isle of Raasay to watch the next phase of the competition.

As soon as the young halflings were far enough away from the pools that she could no longer see the beams of their flashlights shining through the darkness, Guardian Myla flew to the edge of the rocks. She burst to the front of a group of four fae to confront them. They had been watching Mia and her friends while they were at the pool.

"You are not welcome here," she said. "Leave now and never return."

The four didn't seem too concerned with her warning and only snickered at her. Alania and a small group of others flew up to Myla.

"Head Guardian, will you give us permission to remove them?" Alania requested.

Myla agreed with a nod. The other guardians soared over the fae males and sprinkled them with fine, shimmering dust. Immediately, they lifted off their feet and hovered in the air.

"What's happening?" one of them demanded. "What are you doing?"

"We were getting ready to leave," another said. "There's no need to play dirty."

The collection of faerie guardians didn't care about their protests. They giggled and flew higher over the floating men. They took delight in the confusion and fear the intruders showed as they looked around, trying to figure out what was happening. None of them had control over their bodies. They couldn't get themselves back to the ground or even move their arms enough to reach any of the tiny creatures above them. All they could do was continue to argue.

The faerie guardians sprinkled more of the dust over them, which put them completely under the faeries' control. The four fae could do nothing as the guardians flew toward one of the waterfalls, luring the floating men along with them with the enchantment of the spell. Once behind the waterfall, the faeries positioned themselves over a small pool. When the men looked down, all they saw were the rocks jutting out from the sides of the walls covering the water. They were terrified the faerie guardians were about to dash them against those stones.

Instead, the guardians flew sharply toward the water, taking the four fae along with them. At the last moment, they pulled up and used their combined magic to throw the men under the edge of the rocks, and into the water beneath. The fae broke through the surface and down into a very tight portal. Within seconds their screams were gone. The portal claimed them, and there was no one to save them. It took them down into a very dark, isolated place within Faerie.

Carson had been right; there were monsters in some of the portals.

Once the shadows found them, no one would ever see or hear from the four henchmen again.

When the sound of the screams was gone, and the guardians returned, Myla called out to a faerie who was standing at the edge of a pool, staring into the water. "Alania, may I have a word with you?"

The young faerie turned to her and nodded before coming over. "Yes, Head Guardian?" she asked.

"I think you should join your cousin Cinder, and keep an eye on the heir," Myla said. "But keep your reasons quiet. Don't give too much away."

"What should I tell Cinder?" Alania asked. "She knows I am training to be a guardian. She will wonder what I'm doing so far away from the pools."

"Tell her you were granted leave to spend time with her, and to help keep them out of trouble during their time here in Scotland. Offer yourself as their tour guide. Your cousin doesn't spend much time here, does she?"

"No," Alania admitted. "She much prefers to be at the academy."

"Perfect. That means you know the island much better than she does, and certainly better than the halflings. Tell them you will be their tour guide and show them around the island. That one, Luna, seemed very interested in the history of the area. You can give them information and answer their questions. Just watch out for Mia and keep her safe."

Alania nodded and hurried off to join Cinder. Her cousin was staying in the tent with the girls and was surprised when Alania flew through the flap.

"Alania," Cinder said. "What are you doing here? Is everything all right?" Her eyes flashed to Mia and back to her cousin.

"Myla gave me leave from my guardian responsibilities and

training so I can spend more time with you, Cinder. I thought you might like to have a tour guide." Alania smiled as she said it, hoping she was convincing. She thought they may be suspicious, but the girls were immediately excited.

"That would be fantastic!" Luna gushed.

"She could help us with our papers," Mia added.

"Oh, now you're excited about having someone help you with your work," Luna teased, and Mia tossed a pillow at her playfully.

"It could be really great," Vivi said. "She can show us things other people don't know about. Imagine all the possibilities."

Cinder looked at each of the girls, then back at her cousin. She nodded.

"Thanks. That could be fun."

CHAPTER EIGHTEEN

Narco stormed angrily through his study, his mind racing and his hands tingling with the fury rushing through him. He couldn't believe he hadn't heard anything yet. He had sent his henchmen out far too long ago to not have heard anything back from them. He had reached out to them, wanting an update on their patrols around the Slamball World Championships, searching for Mia and the others. But he'd heard nothing, and the longer he waited, the angrier he became.

He hated having to rely on other people while he sat around and waited for them to get back to him. It drove him to the edge of his sanity. There was nothing he could do about it right now. There was no way he could show himself at the games. Far too many people were looking for him. He would stand out and be captured. He had sent people he thought would provide him with information he could use.

"This is ridiculous!" he shouted, sweeping his arm across his desk to knock away the papers piled there. "How am I supposed to get anything done if they can't manage a simple task?"

Narco needed someone he trusted to be his eyes and ears at the games. They were swarming with students, and nothing would keep Mia away from them. If he could find out what she and her friends were doing and follow their patterns, he could finally capture and deliver her and complete the mission that had been hanging over him for so long.

But everyone he had sent kept failing him. None had been able to give him even the smallest bit of useful information, and every minute that ticked by reminded him of the meeting with the man in the shadows. The man's words kept repeating in Narco's mind, and he grew more anxious.

Finally, he couldn't take the waiting any longer. His henchmen weren't going to give him the update he needed and were doing him no good.

"If you want something done right, you have to do it yourself," he muttered.

He thought through the situation for several minutes, using what he knew about the championships and Mia to put together a glamour he thought might help him. It was compelling and made him look different at a glance.

But if anyone was to look too closely or know what they were looking for, they would see past it. The only thing he had going for him was that the weaker halflings couldn't see past glamours. As long as he could stay clear of officials, and any of the full fae who might be there, he would likely be fine.

It would at least give him some time to find her and put himself in a position to watch her. Once he found her, it would be a matter of not making himself obvious. There would be so many people at the games that he hoped to blend in with them and remain among the halflings who wouldn't recognize him.

If he stayed to the shadows and didn't draw too much attention to himself, he could keep an eye on Mia.

But he couldn't leave for the championships yet. Before he went to the games, he had something else to do. The need for proof for his boss hadn't left his mind. He still hadn't come up with any other means of proof besides DNA. Which meant he had to get Mia's hairbrush. He was going to take hair from it to use for her DNA. Once he had it, he could prove her heritage.

First, he wanted to make sure he was on the right track. Without the updates he had requested, he couldn't be sure the halflings were where he thought they were. He couldn't imagine Mia willingly giving up the chance to go to the World Slamball Championships with her friends.

Yet, when he thought about it longer, he realized that might be exactly why she wouldn't go. Anyone would know she was going to be there, and that's where she would be most easily found. Elmhurst had put extensive security on her already, and it wouldn't surprise Narco if he found out she forbade the girl from being there on the weekends when the chaos would make her the most vulnerable.

When last he knew of her whereabouts, she was in Scotland, but he needed to check again before he went to find her brush. He didn't want to arrive on campus at the academy and find that she was still there. Narco prepared all he needed and then returned to his study to create a portal. With a tap of his hand, it appeared on the wall. He needed little effort to create the portal and here, unlike near the campus, no one could monitor his movements.

Stepping through the portal brought him to Scotland. Once there, he used the skills that made him a formidable bounty hunter to track the group of halflings. The games hadn't yet started for the day, so he had to search the area. He finally found them in the small village of Portree on the Isle of Skye.

Narco watched them from a distance. He was very familiar with the small island, though he wasn't allowed to visit there. As a full fae, he wasn't permitted to set foot on the island when he wasn't in disguise. But he knew Portree well enough to know that the small village always drew the attention of those visiting.

The faeries were often stingy in their willingness to give permission to anyone wanting to come to their island, but occasionally they felt generous. Sometimes, when they were feeling celebratory or nostalgic, they would give more people permission to come. Those were the times when Narco had managed to sneak onto the island in disguise.

It never lasted for long. The faeries could recognize intruders, and he made it a point to spend only long enough on the island to experience bits of it, but not long enough to get onto the bad side of the guardians there.

Portree was quite small but had everything visitors wanted. Historical sites and stops set up purely for the entertainment of those passing through always brought in crowds. Dotted among them were tiny shops, bakeries, and booths, overflowing with delicious foods.

Narco heard Luna scolding Carson for eating so much, reminding him they were going to the games later, and he would be too full to enjoy it. The Unseelie boy assured her he would happily enjoy the games, and by then would have plenty of room to stuff himself with more of the snacks available there.

Seeing Mia so close, and not being able to grab her, was torturous. Narco was so near her that he could have snatched her, and taken her through a portal before anyone would have had the chance to react. It took all his control to stop himself. For so long, he had searched for her. So many times he had believed he had found and finished her. But every time he had been wrong. Now he couldn't just act. He had to wait for approval, for confirmation. She was right there, but he had to wait. At least now he knew for sure where she was, and that she wouldn't be on campus to thwart his plan.

Narco found a place where no one would notice him and created a portal to the academy campus. The restrictions on the school ensured that he was unable to simply appear within the building, as he would have preferred.

It would have been so much easier to create a portal directly to the dorm building and go up to her room. But there were enchantments and spells in place to stop that from happening. Instead, he had to use the same place he had used several times before, arriving on the edge of the grounds.

While the campus did have certain protections from anyone creating un-sanctioned portals, there wasn't anything to stop him from *walking* onto campus. As long as he entered with confidence, and acted as though he belonged there, no one would give him a second look.

He didn't bother to use a tremendous amount of caution. The chances of him being caught were slim to none. It was morning in Scotland, which meant that, with the time-zone difference, it was the middle of the night in Montana. Everything was quiet, and the very few students who weren't in Scotland were in bed asleep.

He was able to climb over the wall and onto the academy grounds easily. He was still using his glamour, which meant he could roam around as if he belonged, and the students would have no idea who he was. He strode right through the campus without a care and headed directly for the dorms.

CHAPTER NINETEEN

Morning would be coming in a few hours, but for now, the sun wasn't up. That meant Dan and Steve were still free from their pedestals and flying around campus, keeping an eye on things. These nightly outings had taken on more meaning for them when the championships started, and students were leaving the grounds in droves.

So many people were gone from the campus that it felt less secure and protected. They both believed there should be more security, ensuring the buildings and grounds were protected and guarded, even when there weren't as many students there.

"I don't understand why Elmhurst doesn't make sure there are guards in place during the night," Steve worried as they glided together over the library in a low loop. "So many students and teachers have left the grounds, it feels like it's leaving the academy wide open for anyone to come."

"There should definitely be more security," Dan said, swinging his head back and forth so he could scan as much of the surrounding area as possible as they flew. "I know it's Saturday night, but that doesn't matter. She should understand that is what's making the school vulnerable. While everyone is off enjoying the games in Scotland, the school is sitting here unprotected, and anything could happen."

"You're right. What if someone came in and stole from the library?" Steve asked. "There are some priceless books and artifacts in there. Someone could take something that couldn't ever be replaced. Or that has information in it no one wants in the wrong hands."

"Well, what if someone went into one of the school buildings, and broke all the equipment in the classrooms? Then when the students came back for class, they wouldn't have any way to do their lessons," Dan said.

"Without anybody around to watch the buildings and keep them secure, someone could sneak in and plant a bomb that blows up the whole building," Steve offered. "It could destroy part of the campus."

"What if they set a booby trap specifically for Mia and no one noticed, and she got hurt? Or snatched?" Dan asked.

They were building on each other, escalating to increasingly bigger and bigger problems the more they talked about what could possibly happen. Which made them more and more worried and anxious because they couldn't do much other than patrol the area and watch for anything happening. They both wished they could do more, and their conversation drifted back, as it often did, to their inability to leave their posts during the day. It would have been more beneficial if they could go out and provide additional surveillance when the students were more likely to be on campus.

Because of the time difference with Scotland, the students drifted on- and off-campus at all times. The rules mandated they were there for their classes during the week, but then they could go to the games in the evenings. When the weekends came, they could spend more time there. It made the gargoyles more nervous when it was a day without a senior high championship game. That meant the students were scattered across the country, making it harder to gather them and protect them if necessary.

On days when there was no high school match, there was usually a major league slamball game to attend. Unlike the high school games, tickets to the major-league meets weren't guaranteed and were harder to come by. Everyone wanted to watch the impressive spectacle of the professional players and cheer on their favorite team.

Tickets had to be distributed by lottery. Only those whose names were selected were given the opportunity to buy the tickets. Not only did that make the game exclusive and more desirable, but it meant those who didn't win had more free time. They weren't about to give up their chance to tour Scotland and connect with other fae students. Instead, they spread out through the country and its islands.

This was especially an issue today. The major league game taking place next to Arthur's Seat, on the edge of Edinburgh, was a heated rivalry. It wasn't only the students who swarmed to Scotland to see the game. The majority of the faculty had gone to watch their favorite league players battle each other to settle the bid for supremacy for another season.

For Dan and Steve, that just meant fewer people on campus to monitor things. They had to pick up the slack and keep watch over as much of the academy grounds and its surrounding areas as they possibly could.

CHAPTER TWENTY

Narco could see the dark shadows of the creatures flying overhead. He knew who they were and what they were doing. Having few people on campus was an advantage for him. It meant less chance to be seen. But the gargoyles could be a problem.

He couldn't let them see him. The bounty hunter measured his movements by the way the two flew around the sky. They could only cover a certain area at a time, which meant there were stretches when his way was clear. They hovered near the dorms for several long minutes, almost as though they sensed something was wrong, then parted ways to go to other points on the grounds.

As soon as both were out of sight, Narco rushed into the girls' dorm. It took little time or effort to find where Mia and the other two girls of the Five lived. Just as he expected, the three were given special treatment, with a more elaborate room than the standard ones. The smaller rooms only accommodated two girls. This room, with its prime position within the building and bigger space, ensured the three were forced into spending more time together. It was, by design, melding their lives together to increase their power.

Narco took a deep breath as he walked into the room and looked around. He pulled his magic forward, calling on his gift of bringing stories to life to conjure the image of the last person to use objects within the room. Going to each of the bedside tables, he focused on the brushes and combs sitting there.

The table next to the bed nearest the door held an assortment of four brushes arranged across it. For a moment, Narco thought maybe all the girls kept their things together, but then the image in his mind proved they all belonged to Vivi. He rolled his eyes at the vanity of the Unseelie girl. Next, he moved on to a table with one comb. The strand of hair tangled in it was lighter, and he envisioned Luna using it. That meant the last table had to belong to Mia.

Narco walked up to the table but didn't see a brush or comb lying there. He opened the drawer and found nothing helpful. She must have taken her only brush with her when she went to Scotland. He was feeling discouraged until he turned to her bed, and an idea came to mind. It was neatly made, the blankets and sheets tucked around the pillow and smoothed perfectly into place. He carefully loosened one corner and folded it away from the pillow. A smile slithered across his face when he saw the pillowcase. Just as he hoped, several strands of long red hair clung to the white fabric.

He reached into the inner pocket of his jacket and retrieved a small bag he had brought along for the occasion. Carefully picking up the hairs, he tucked them into the bag and returned it to his pocket. He took them all, knowing that not all hair came out with the follicles intact. With extra strands, he was confident there would be enough to extract DNA for his testing needs.

Then he put the blankets back in place and headed for the door. Feeling triumphant, he casually sauntered back outside and headed across the school grounds.

He was almost at the wall when Steve and Dan caught sight of him. They rushed across the sky but weren't in time to stop him. They watched as he created a portal beyond the grounds, and strode through it, disappearing in a flash. Eyes wide, they looked at each other.

"That was Narco," Steve said. "He's come back to the academy."

"What was he doing here?" Dan asked.

Steve shook his head. "I don't know, but we have to tell the headmistress. Right now."

"We need to make sure that new wards go up to keep out evil fae." Steve always hated that anyone could walk on campus. That seemed dangerous, as well as stupid. He never understood why they controlled portal usage on-campus, but didn't control who came and went beyond the gates of the academy.

CHAPTER TWENTY-ONE

Trying as hard as they could to not panic, Dan and Steve flew to Elmhurst's office. They were in such a state of worry it didn't enter their minds that it was the middle of the night, and the headmistress wouldn't be sitting at her desk the way she often was after sunset most evenings. She loved her academy and was devoted to her position, but not enough to sleep in the big chair in the office. They reached the window where they often paused to talk to her and peered inside. Her office was dark, so they soared off to her private quarters.

Elmhurst lived in the same ancient impressive quarters as her ancestor, who had created the academy centuries ago. It looked like the interior of a castle, all heavy stone draped with tapestries. She had done a few things to add her own personality to the space and lighten it up, but for the most part, had left it as it was when she had moved in. It was tradition and part of the prestige of holding the position of headmistress.

Dan and Steve glided right to the large curved window of her bedroom and landed on the rounded stone edge of a small balcony. They looked in through the glass, but they didn't see anything. It was dark inside, and there were no candles or lights burning anywhere. It was only after they flew around the building, and looked into every window they could find, that they remembered she, too, was off-campus.

Elmhurst was a huge fan of Slamball, and her favorite team was playing in the major league game at Arthur's Seat. She had entered the lottery as soon as it was announced, and had been thrilled to be able to scoop up tickets.

But that meant she wasn't there for them to tell her about Narco. They rushed around campus, checking the buildings, looking into windows, trying to find someone they could notify about the intrusion. Not all the faculty and staff were viable options. Some only knew the most essential basics of the situation because of their limited abilities, or their connections and alliances outside the academy. It wasn't that Elmhurst didn't trust them, but for some, their families and friends in Faerie could become problematic if they revealed too much.

The gargoyles couldn't find anyone to tell, and the night was slipping away. It wouldn't be too much longer before the sun came up, and there would be nothing more they could do. They had no choice but to notify Elmhurst in Scotland.

She had given them a communication stone that allowed them to instantly connect to her. It was much more reliable than any other form of communication when she was at a distance, especially in another country. They activated the stone and waited.

The game was reaching a fever pitch, and Elmhurst was buzzing with excitement when the communication stone around her neck warmed against her skin. The feeling instantly dampened her spirits and tightened her muscles with concern. Steve and Dan knew using the stone was only for truly urgent situations. Especially today as she took an extremely rare break from campus and everything going on there to enjoy herself and watch her favorite team.

She reached under her jacket and pulled out the stone. It hung from a chain around her neck that was long enough for her to hold the stone in her palm and look at it. Pressing the glowing depression in the middle of the stone, she activated the message sent by the gargoyles. There was only one word. Narco.

Elmhurst scrambled to her feet, rushed from the stadium, and ran to a secure location to create a portal back to the academy. Watching carefully around her to ensure no one was about who might try to enter the portal with her, she jumped through to the school. Dan and Steve were waiting outside the window to her office, and she opened it to let them in.

"What happened?" she asked, worried.

Both statues burst into an elaborate story of what they saw.

"He had to be planting a bomb."

"He's going to sabotage the whole school."

"Maybe he took someone hostage and made them invisible."

"Narco is so dangerous, he probably rigged the entire school to trap Mia and all the other students as soon as they get back."

She held up her hands to silence them. "One at a time. Tell me what actually happened," she said. "Not what you *think* could happen. Not guesses. What actually happened?"

They described Narco crossing the school grounds, and then going through a portal. A chill ran along her spine. Elmhurst had hoped they were imagining things or were coming up with some wild idea, but now she knew it was serious.

"I'm going to recall all the faculty, and get Cassia here. We need to secure the campus," she announced. "There is still some time before the sun comes up here. Keep watch over the grounds, especially the borders. Tell me immediately if you see anything."

Dan and Steve nodded their acknowledgment and flew out of the window into the night. Seconds later, Cassia appeared at the door. She looked worried as she rushed up to the desk. "What happened?" she asked.

Elmhurst explained the situation. "Do you know where Mia is at this very moment?" she asked when she finished.

Cassia reached into the leather satchel she wore over her shoulder and pulled out a mirror. "I put a spell on this mirror to keep me connected to her," she explained. She activated the mirror and held it out to the headmistress. "Here."

Elmhurst took the mirror and looked at the glass. Color rippled across the surface for a second before clearing and showing an image. Mia walked along with Zander, Luna, Carson, and Vivi. They seemed happy and carefree as they strolled along a narrow road, eating ice cream. Mia looked at Zander and laughed before they went into one of the little shops lining the street.

"They're in Portree," Elmhurst said with a relieved sigh. "They're safe. Cinder is with them. And the faeries control the island. They wouldn't allow someone like Narco in their territory."

She relaxed slightly, relieved to see the five having fun and not concerned about anything.

"Good. I always liked the Isle of Skye faeries." She chuckled.

"What should we do now?" Cassia asked, taking the mirror back and looking down at the image.

"For right now, they don't know anything is amiss. There's no reason to worry them yet. It's best for them to stay where they are and continue enjoying themselves while we search the campus and make sure it's safe. Once we know more about what he was doing here, we can decide what needs to be done," Elmhurst said.

The faculty and staff Elmhurst recalled from Scotland filtered into the building, and she gathered them in one of the larger meeting rooms. They divided up the campus and planned out how they were to methodically search the grounds. It was critical no corner was missed, no detail overlooked. The smallest thing could be an indication of something much larger. Every single room needed to be checked, every inch of the grounds had to be searched. It was a massive undertaking, but with all of the faculty, staff, and extra security working together, they managed to do it.

Two hours later, they had found nothing out of the ordinary. While a few of the teams went over the outer sections of the grounds again, Elmhurst returned to her office to meet with Steve and Dan.

"Are you absolutely sure you saw Narco?" she asked. "You know it was him?"

"Yes," Dan insisted. "It was him."

"We swear. We wouldn't cause this much trouble if we didn't know for sure it was him," Steve added.

Elmhurst nodded. "I know. The only thing left to do is look at the security cameras. They don't have full coverage, but they might show us something. Of course, if he knew they were there, nothing is going to stop Narco from concealing himself, and his activities."

It was a last-resort effort. Searching the grounds to eliminate any immediate threat was the most important thing to do first. But since they hadn't found anything, it was time to dig deeper. She pulled up the footage from the camera and watched it closely. Several panels on the screen showed the feed from all the different cameras positioned around campus.

"I don't see him anywhere," she said a few minutes later.

Cassia leaned over her shoulder, and they watched the footage again. The bounty hunter suddenly pointed at the screen. "Look right there," she said. "That's a glamour."

Elmhurst couldn't believe she hadn't spotted it when she watched the video the first time. It was convincing, and glamours were much more difficult to see through over cameras than they were in person. Now that she knew what she was looking at, it was obvious. There he was.

They watched Narco move across the grounds and into the dorm. Elmhurst and Cassia looked at each other.

"Was the dorm searched?" Elmhurst asked.

"Yes, but only quickly," Cassia said. "Nothing seemed to be moved anywhere in the building, and the team didn't want to waste any time."

Elmhurst nodded, understanding the decision, but knowing they had less time to waste now. "We need to search it more deeply. He could have done something that isn't noticeable at just a glance."

CHAPTER TWENTY-TWO

"I will put a protective spell on the dorm," Elmhurst said, standing. "It will prevent anyone from getting out, and anyone unauthorized from getting in."

"Good idea," Cassia said, "I'll take a couple of my friends, and we'll go search the dorm and see if we can see anything. They're bounty hunters, and can use their skills to help."

Elmhurst nodded and the two walked to the dorms, splitting up when they reached the main entrance. The principal stood stoically as she conjured the spell that would envelop the dorm in a protective bubble, impenetrable by anyone who wasn't expressly allowed in.

As powerful as she was, it only took total concentration for a few moments to conjure it, but Cassia knew she would want to be thorough. Elmhurst would likely go through a sealing process that would take a few more minutes to complete, giving her spell a sort of authentication double-check.

While the principal took care of the bubble, Cassia met with the three bounty-hunter friends she had called on for the job. Often, bounty hunters were distrustful of anyone and everyone, including other bounty hunters. If one day you ran afoul of someone powerful, your colleagues would likely be the ones sent to find you, so you kept mostly to yourself. But still, there was always a loose network of hunters who tended to remain friendly, if nothing else other than for the ability to call in help if a hunter realized they were in over their head. Considering Cassia wasn't entirely sure what she was up against, calling in these three made the most sense for her.

"Carl," said the lone woman of the three, a thin fae with sharp bone-structure, and a long nose that made her resemble a hawk. "She's here." The woman, Valerie, tapped her husband on the shoulder, and he turned to see Cassia coming.

"Ahh, Cassia," said the portly man.

Valerie's husband, Carl, was a legend in the bounty-hunting community, primarily for a string of jobs he had done in his youth that had nabbed him a great deal of fame and fortune. He was skilled and experienced, more so than most anyone else Cassia knew besides herself. Carl wasn't much of a field guy anymore, though, as evidenced by the belly now hanging over the belt of his pants, but Cassia had no doubt that in a moment of action, he would be ready.

Valerie, his wife and fellow bounty-hunter, was less famous, but perhaps better than he was. She was fast, athletic, and exceptionally smart. Cassia had met them when she had still been learning the ropes of bounty hunting, and they had become very close mentors for her.

"Are we ready?" asked the stick-figure of a man on the other side of Valerie.

If Valerie was a thin woman, Warren was nearly two-dimensional. His seemingly nervous disposition hid the fact that he was a brilliant detective. On more than one occasion, when Cassia lost track of a target, Warren had been the one to save her hide.

"We are. I'll pull up the last twenty-four hours and see if we can find out what happened before doing a deep search," Cassia said.

As the four bounty hunters walked into the main hall, Cassia began the motions required to use the spell. With it, Cassia could create an image of the last twenty-four hours of any space, and wind through it at will. Casting it around her would allow her and her associates to watch as the day unfolded around them, ghosts of the students and faculty going around and through them as they sped through time. If there was someone worth following, they could simply walk the path that the person trod and check what they did and where they went, provided it was within the space the spell was being cast.

"Who are we looking for?" Valerie asked, as the images popping up around them, mostly transparent people, came to a stop twenty-four hours earlier. They were standing in the main hall, which was crowded with apparitions.

"I am trying to find Mia and the rest of her little gang first," Cassia explained. "If I can find them, I can see if anything out of the ordinary was going on around them yesterday. Failing that, we are looking for Narco, who was using a pretty poor glamour. Should be easy enough to spot."

A few minutes passed as Cassia went around the room, looking into the transparent faces of all the students. When she couldn't find Mia or any of the others, she motioned for the bounty hunters to join her, and they walked up to the girls' rooms. With Warren and Carl remaining on the floor below, Cassia and Valerie went onto the next floor. Cassia checked the shower room first, and, finding it empty, moved down the hall.

"Her room is just ahead. At this time of the day, she should be in there asleep," Cassia said as if trying to convince herself Mia would be there. Something was nagging at her. She had a bad feeling about what she was going to find when the door opened. Sure enough, when Cassia turned the knob and went inside, the room was empty.

She knew the girls were in Portree, but that didn't mean she hadn't hoped they would have come home by now, and be safely tucked away in bed. "Let's just do the time-lapse to last night. I want to see what, if anything, Narco did in here."

The spell caught up to just a few hours before, and Cassia stopped as the doorknob turned. As they watched, the door swung open, and a shimmery, unconvincing glamor—hiding Narco underneath—entered the room. Cassia watched him in confusion as he went around the room, looking through drawers.

"Well, that's creepy," Valerie said, as he picked up a comb that lay on Luna's bedside table, and tossed it down. Narco went to Mia's bed, knelt on one knee, and pulled something from his pocket. It was a plastic bag. Cassia watched in horror as he picked up a few strands of hair and put them in the bag.

"Oh, that good-for-nothing roasted cricket," Cassia said under her breath.

"That can't be good," Valerie said.

They watched Narco leave the room and followed him down the stairs, walking past Carl and Warren.

"Is that the guy?" Warren asked as the glamour-bound spectral image passed him.

"Yes," Cassia said through gritted teeth. "And he took some of Mia's hair."

"What would he want that for? A spell?" Warren scratched his chin.

Cassia didn't answer. Of course, it could be for a spell. That was the easy option. The alternative was worse; That Narco had figured out who Mia was, and was aiming to prove it. Either way, Mia was in deep trouble.

The portal opened outside the coffee shop, and Cassia, Elmhurst, and the three other bounty hunters walked into Portree as the five halflings were exiting the cafe. They stumbled in surprise.

Without a moment's hesitation, Carson passed his cup to

Luna, put his hands behind his back, and took a neutral pose. Taking his inspiration from Zander, lawyering Carson had turned the spotlight on himself, and Elmhurst was not amused.

"To what do we owe the pleasure of such a...well-attended visit?" Carson said, looking at the three bounty hunters and then at Mia, who shrugged.

"None of you slept in your dorm room last night. We checked. That's against school rules," Cassia said, her eyes stabbing into Mia, who winced.

"Well," Carson began, suddenly looking relaxed and argumentative at the same time. He was now embodying every slick lawyer in every crime-drama TV show in the history of time. "Technically speaking, we were given permission to be in Scotland for *the weekend*," he said, his fingers doing air quotes around the last two words. "As it is still the weekend, we are not due back yet. Nowhere was it said that we needed to sleep there. Arrangements were all set up here, and are on the up and up. The boys stayed in one tent and the girls in another. No harm, no foul."

"That is where you are seriously mistaken," Elmhurst told him.

CHAPTER TWENTY-THREE

"You know very well you aren't allowed to sleep anywhere but your assigned dorm rooms without written permission," Elmhurst said firmly. "That is a rule of the academy you learn from the moment you are granted admission and is in force at all times. Luna, who lives nearby, can't just go home for the weekend with her mother without permission from the school. That is done for the safety and security of each of our students. I need to know where you are at all times. That rule does not change just because of the special circumstances of the World Slamball Championships. There are already many concessions being made, and special privileges being granted because of the games. But that is not one of them. You know that. All of you know that."

Cassia shook her head as she looked at Mia. Her eyes were heavy, and the halfling could see the dark emotion on her guardian's face.

"I am so disappointed in you, Mia," Cassia said. "You know the rules. We've talked about them. Just because you are allowed to go visit Scotland for the championships, doesn't mean you don't have to adhere to the rest of the rules of campus. That includes sleeping only in your assigned room each night."

Mia hung her head. She felt guilty for her part in the weekend. She had known she was agreeing to something that wasn't right when Zander had first suggested it. The time difference made it hard to keep up with a normal sleep-wake cycle between the two places, but she had known when they did sleep, it was supposed to be in their dorms.

"I'm sorry," she said. "I just got wrapped up in the excitement of going."

Elmhurst shook her head again. She caught sight of a small faerie hovering near the group. "You," she said, looking at the creature sternly. "You are a guardian-in-training for the faerie pools. What are you doing here?"

"Yes," Alania replied. "I am. My name is Alania. I was granted a break from my training and responsibilities at the pools to visit with my cousin, Cinder."

Elmhurst raised an eyebrow, not saying anything as she thought the response through. Then she gave a single nod. "Very good," she said. She turned to the group of halflings. "We are going back to the school. Immediately."

All five nodded solemnly, saddened to have lost the carefree fun of exploring the village together. They didn't want to be back on the academy campus, away from the games and the festivities. But in a situation like this, there wasn't going to be any leniency. Elmhurst escorted them to an isolated area behind a building and created a portal to the academy. It brought them directly into the girls' dorm room, so there would be no argument about where they needed to go.

When they arrived, the headmistress looked pointedly at each of the halflings. "Listen closely. Your rules have now changed. You are no longer permitted free access to Scotland and the Championships. You are to stay on campus unless you have an adult with you, and you must have that adult with you at all times."

The five sagged, exchanging pained looks, sulking over their lost freedom. They understood the gravity of the situation they were facing, but none of them wanted to. Going to the games and exploring Scotland was a way for them to not have to worry so much, and to relax and have fun. Now they had been forced back into being constantly monitored and controlled.

Alania saw how upset they were, and flitted a bit closer to Elmhurst. "Headmistress, if I may? Cinder and I are adults. We can supervise the children if they want to continue to spend their free time in Scotland," she offered.

The halflings couldn't help but laugh at the idea of the faeries being their chaperones, but Cassia gave them a sharp glare, instantly silencing them. Elmhurst studied the faerie, evaluating her words. Alania was not just a faerie making a generous offer to allow these students freedom from campus. There was more going on here than met the eye. But this wasn't the time to question it.

Elmhurst nodded. "If you can arrange for you and two of your guardian sisters to stay with the children the entire time they are in Scotland, that is acceptable." She turned to the students and pointed at them, making sure they were listening and would fully understand her. "But you must sleep in your own beds here at the academy, in your dorm rooms. And you will now have a curfew that must be met on all occasions, no exceptions. During the week, you have to be in all of your classes, do all your work, and attend all extracurricular activities, meetings, and events required of you. If you miss anything, you will not be permitted to go to Scotland that day. You will not be permitted to leave until all classes and activities for the day are done, even if you have met the requirements for the day. Every weekday, you will be back on campus no later than ten. That is still very early morning by Scotland time, so it will give you plenty of opportunity to sleep before the next events begin."

"We can accept that," Zander said, returning to his self-appointed post as the group's quasi-leader.

"You don't have any choice, Zander. This is not a negotiation, it is a declaration of terms. This is the only option you have. On weekends, you will have a bit more freedom. You can leave first thing in the morning, assuming there are no seminars or extended coursework assigned. Your curfew is midnight."

They nodded, and Elmhurst began to leave the room to return to her office. Before she went too far, she glanced over her shoulder at them. "All stated times are Montana time. I don't want to hear you thought the curfew was midnight, Scotland time."

It was the last little bit of hope a few of the five had been holding out. The headmistress hadn't been specific, which had meant they might get away with a little bit of wiggle room. With that stipulation, though, their hopes of stretching out their time in Scotland were dashed. Deflated, they all nodded again and mumbled their agreements.

Elmhurst took two steps before saying, "Alania, a word." She walked far enough away that the halflings wouldn't hear their conversation. Someone needed to know that Narco was around, and she wanted to know what Alania knew.

"I told you it wasn't going to work," Carson grumbled, kicking the floor.

"You did not," Mia corrected him. "You were just as enthusiastic about camping on the Isle of Skye as Zander was. Luna is the only one who was really resistant to it, and said we shouldn't do it."

"All of you should have known better," Cassia said. "And if one of you was arguing against it, you should have listened."

Luna sighed and threw her hands up in the air. "And yet, I did it anyway, and look where it got me. Why do I always go along with all of you?" she asked.

"You have to," Vivi teased. "It's the Power of Five, not four."

The joke helped to lighten the mood slightly, and they all laughed. They still felt discouraged. They had only gotten the chance to camp out in their tents for one night, and all of them had enjoyed it. Even the girls had relaxed and had started having fun.

There was something exhilarating about being in such a different environment, doing something out of their usual routine. They always slept in the same space, and the elevated tent had brought them into closer proximity with each other, but it still felt fun and exciting. They had enjoyed being around the other visitors, and feeling like they were a part of it all.

Being students from the number-one-rated school in the World Slamball Championships was a rare and special thing. Something they had had the opportunity to experience once, and this was it. Now, instead of being among all the other revelers, fully immersed in the thrill, they were stuck on campus, imagining everything they were missing out on.

But at least they had Alania, and her offer to supervise them when they wanted to go. They didn't have to ask one of the teachers to come with them or try to find a parent willing to do the traveling.

It was a kind and generous offer, but it also made Mia wonder. She waited for Alania to return to their room, and for Cassia to say goodbye and leave, before turning to the faerie, who stared back at her.

CHAPTER TWENTY-FOUR

"Alania, why would you offer to supervise us?" Mia asked. "You said you were given permission to take time away from your training and guardian duties to visit with Cinder, not to watch over us."

The faerie shrugged. She didn't want to tell them the truth and let them know what was actually going on. Head Guardian Myla had asked her, in confidence, to keep an eye on Mia. If Myla had wanted all of them to know about it, she would have asked Alania to do it in front of them. Alania wanted to protect that confidence, and not let them know she was actually there to watch over the heir.

"Guarding the pools, and training with the other guardians isn't a lot of fun sometimes. My friends and I would find it much more exciting to hang out with you guys, attend the games, and go sightseeing." Her tiny shoulders lifted, and she rolled her eyes. "Think of it as a human vacation."

That made sense to Mia. The faeries at the pools seemed to be having fun playing in the water, and the surroundings were beautiful and exciting when the halflings had first seen them. But it was probably different when those pools were a part of their everyday life, and they were tasked with protecting them.

Knowing they had hundreds, or even thousands, of years ahead of them at the pools every day, guarding them against people, and people from them, likely took some of the novelty away.

It would be like the time her human high school class went to a theme park for a field trip close to the end of the year. They had all believed it was going to be a fun day of riding rides and running around celebrating the end of the year together. But when they stepped off the bus at the front of the park, they were promptly met with thick packets of worksheets which they were expected to fill out during their time in the park. Having to analyze the rides, and answer seemingly endless questions about them, their themes, how they worked, what was good and what wasn't, had made the day seem much more like another boring school assignment than anything exciting.

The games were an infrequent event, even for the faeries, and would present an opportunity to see a lot of new things. It made sense that they would jump at the chance to change up their routine for a few days.

Mia and the Scooby Gang bought the explanation, but Cinder didn't. She had watched the interaction between Mia and Alania and knew something more was going on. She wanted to question her cousin, but before she could, Zander stood.

"I think we should go to the library," he announced.

Vivi groaned and toppled backward onto her bed. "I am so not in the mood to do more research."

"Not for research. I want to hear what Dan and Steve have to say about all this. All we know is what Elmhurst and Cassia told us. Maybe the gargoyles can give us a different perspective," he told them.

"Or at least a really entertaining story," Carson said.

The girls agreed, and Mia beckoned Alania. "Come on," she

said. "We'll introduce you to Dan and Steve, the resident gargoyles."

"Where are they?" Alania asked, as they left the dorm room, and strolled across the grounds to the library.

"They are stationed outside the library," Mia explained. "They've been there since the academy was built more than one thousand years ago."

"If they are gargoyles, how did they manage to see anything?" the faerie asked. "Wouldn't they only be able to see what is immediately around them?"

"That's the way it used to be. Until Mia started feeling bad for them and managed to enchant them off their pedestals. Now they're able to fly around from sundown to sunup. They can go around and do pretty much whatever they like, but as soon as the sun comes up, they have to go back to their posts," Vivi told them.

"That doesn't sound like fun. At least there's nothing locking me to the pools," the faerie said.

"Yeah, they're pretty grumpy about it. It's like they forgot they didn't even know they could move for hundreds and hundreds of years. Now, all of a sudden, they get frustrated because they have to stay in place for a few hours at a time," the Unseelie halfling told them.

"But they make the most of the time they can be free," Mia said. "They like to keep watch over the campus and make sure everything is all right. They could go anywhere and do anything, but they still want to stay here and keep watch over the academy. And it's a good thing they do."

They reached the library, and Dan and Steve strained, as though trying to lean down toward the halflings.

"We're so glad to see you," Dan said.

"Tell us what happened. What's going on?" Zander asked.

The gargoyles burst into their hyped-up story and the

halflings smiled at each other, ready to settle in and try to sift through the exaggerations to find what really happened.

Narco stood in the hidden room in front of a long table cluttered with chemistry equipment. He had gathered everything he needed to combine magic and science and draw the DNA from Mia's hair. If he could obtain a breakdown of it, he could then compare it to that of the royal line, and prove once and for all that she was the girl they were after. That is if his contact could procure a DNA sample from the Unseelie Queen.

He wasn't worried about that part. If his contact wanted proof, then Narco would give him the sample, and tell him he could compare it himself if proof was so important to him.

But Narco's efforts weren't going smoothly.

He picked up another piece of hair and slid it into a test tube. He poured in an enchanted solution and went through the process, which should have revealed all the secrets of who she was.

But within seconds of the solution touching the hair, the strand disintegrated with a *poof*. This was the third time it had happened. He picked up another strand and carefully went through the process again. And again, the hair disappeared. He was no scientist, and his understanding of exactly what he was doing was shaky at best, but Narco knew that wasn't right. He was down to his final strand of hair. If he lost this piece, he would have nothing left, and his chance at presenting proof would be gone.

He growled and felt like throwing the entire desk across the room. He barely managed to restrain himself, and he began to tell himself he could do this. He was Narco, the most revered bounty hunter ever. No one could best him.

He had killed that frustrating Flynn Terran who had believed *he* was the best bounty hunter in a hundred generations. If only Narco could tell all of Faerie that he was the one who killed their favorite hunter. Maybe, once this issue was done, he could let a few stories out about how he was instrumental in ensuring the two Courts were protected. Then he'd have the glory he was due.

Setting the hair on the counter far from the solution, he reached out to the associate who had walked him through the process, to begin with. Several minutes later, a portal appeared in the wall, and his colleague stepped out. A scientist with experience in this process, Orin, listened to Narco's description of what was happening to the hair when he had attempted to withdraw the DNA.

"I am doing what you told me to, just as you told me to do it," Narco insisted. "The same thing keeps happening. It can't be what I'm doing. I think there might be something wrong with the hair."

"You're right. That sounds like someone put a spell on the hair. It's rarely done, but there are enchantments that can be placed on living beings to make it so no DNA can be extracted from things that fall off them, like hair or skin cells. You won't be able to get any DNA from strands of hair, or anything that comes off her naturally," Orin told him.

"Then what am I supposed to do?" Narco asked.

"If this girl has been enchanted, the only way you're going to be able to get DNA is from her blood."

Narco liked where this was headed. He had long envisioned his opportunity to draw blood from Mia. But he had to calm himself down. He remembered what the shadow man had said. He was not permitted to harm her until he had obtained proof she was the girl they wanted.

"Is there a way I can do that without being obvious?" Narco asked.

"It's not difficult to get blood, especially from a halfling. I have worked with several bogans who can be discreet. Unlike the redcaps you prefer. They shouldn't have any trouble getting a sample of blood from Mia. I can reach out to them if you'd like me to," Orin said.

Narco met Orin's eyes, his expression serious and firm.

"Get it done."

CHAPTER TWENTY-FIVE

"Now that you've had a few days to think about your assignment, I want to check in with all of you, and find out what you're thinking about," the teacher said in class on Monday.

Some of the students shifted around in their seats uncomfortably. It was obvious they hadn't thought about the writing assignment since walking out of class at the end of the previous week. They'd been far too wrapped up in the Championships, and in exploring Scotland, to think about what they were going to do for their project. It seemed none of the others had thought about the fact that being able to go to Scotland was the perfect opportunity to find a topic, and do in-depth research. She turned her focus directly to the five.

"What about you, Luna? What did you come up with for your research project?" she asked.

"I want to research the faerie pools more. We went to visit them over the weekend, and I had the opportunity to talk to one of the guardians for a while. I got some interesting information about the pools and the history of the surrounding area. I'd like to look more into that," Luna responded.

"Very good. The pools are fascinating. There are a lot of myths and legends revolving around that area. I look forward to reading your insights into those legends and how they connect to the true history of Scotland and the pools." She smiled at Luna and looked at Mia. "How about you, Mia? Is there something in particular about Scotland that stood out to you?"

"Yes," Mia said, nodding. "I want to learn more about Princess Caledona. We found out she was named for the region, and that people thought she had found the Fountain of Youth because she was powerful, and had lived for so long. I'd like to find out more about where she came from, and what happened to her."

"Interesting," the teacher said with a smile. "And you, Vivi?"

Vivi shrugged. "I haven't made up my mind yet. But I wouldn't mind finding some handsome knights to study."

The class laughed, but the teacher wasn't quite as amused by the declaration. She scowled at Vivi, her arms crossed over her chest.

"I expect you to have a topic by the end of the week. A real topic, Vivi," she said.

She moved on to Zander, who was ready to gloss over the issue with Vivi for the teacher.

"I want to study the Roman-Pict battles," he announced.

The teacher looked intrigued. "That's an interesting idea. What about that particular topic got your attention?"

"There was no way the Picts back then could have stood up against the Roman soldiers and succeeded. There had to be fae intervention. I want to find out about that and see if I can trace some of the fae who were involved," he told her.

"That's ambitious. If you were able to accomplish that, the library might be interested in your findings. That could definitely be something that would make your application stand out to the universities."

She winked at him, knowing his ambitions and how hard he was working to get ahead. The competition for the most elite universities was always fierce each year. He wouldn't just be up against the other seniors from Elmhurst. He would also have to stand out from students from all the other schools as well. He needed to make himself as appealing as possible to be accepted, and start working toward his desired position after graduation.

When Zander had first come up with the project involving the fae interference in the Roman and Pict battles, he had secretly hoped it would be compelling enough to be impressive, but he hadn't wanted to say anything. Getting the validation from the teacher was encouraging and made him more excited to continue with the research.

"I know what I want to do," Carson said, raising his hand. "It actually kind of goes along with what Zander is doing."

"Okay, go ahead," the teacher said.

"I want to study *The Highlander*. He had to be fae, or at least a halfling. There is no way a human could survive the kinds of things that happened to him," Carson said.

The class laughed, and the teacher laughed right along with them, though she stopped herself quickly. She didn't want to embarrass Carson. He was a very good student, and it wasn't often he made a serious mistake. Which made this error particularly funny, but it could also make it more humiliating for him.

"Carson, I think you're confused. That's a movie. It wasn't based on a real person," she said gently.

Carson shook his head. "No," he said firmly. "That's not right. The movie was based on a real person. Just like that one about the guy who painted himself blue and ran up into the mountains. It's a real person, and he could only be killed if he was decapitated. That can't be human."

"Carson," Luna said, shaking her head. "It's not a real person."

"It's true, buddy," Zander said, patting Carson on the shoulder.

Carson looked at the two of them, then at the teacher. After a few seconds he suspended hope, and it puffed out of him in a gusting exhale.

"Well, I guess that means I'm going back to the drawing board for a topic," he said.

The class laughed again as he shrugged.

"We can both study the Roman-Pict battles," Zander suggested. "It's a really big topic. There has to be a lot of fae intervention, and if we're both working on it, we'll be able to find out even more about it."

"That sounds like a fantastic solution," the teacher said. "You two can work together to really dig into this idea and see what you can discover."

Zander and Carson were happy about the decision and immediately delved into talking over the ideas, planning how they were going to move ahead with their research.

When classes were over for the day, the five met up in front of the library. Alania appeared with two of the other guardians in training. Cinder hovered a little behind, seeming to watch her cousin and her friends carefully.

"Are you guys ready?" Alania asked.

The five agreed enthusiastically. They'd been waiting all day for the chance to go back to Scotland and couldn't wait to get there.

"We wish we could go," Steve grumbled.

"Yeah, it's not fair," Dan said. "Everybody else gets to go. We should, too."

"You know the rules," Vivi told them. "When the sun comes up, it's back to your pedestals."

"Exactly. Not fair. I wish Mia could fix it so we don't have to be stuck to the library during the day. We shouldn't have to sit around at all," Dan said.

Mia sighed, frustrated. They had had this exchange a few times already. "I'm sorry, guys. I can't."

"It's not like we want to do anything wrong," Steve told her.

"We just want to stick with you and make sure you're safe. You know we won't fly away. We are loyal to the academy, and to you."

Mia felt tightness in her throat and shook her head. "I'm sorry. I don't know how to do it. I didn't know how to do it when it happened the first time. But I'm practicing with my powers. When I get better and learn more, I can try again. But now, I'm afraid if I try it and don't do it right, I might reverse what I did. And you will be stuck in place forever. Then you wouldn't be able to leave your pedestals at all, not even at night. That's why I want to wait until I have full use and understanding of my powers."

Dan nodded. "I understand. I appreciate you thinking about us."

Steve continued to grumble like a grumpy old man, but it was nice that at least one of them was understanding and appreciative.

"You know, I'd be happy to try," Vivi said, with an evil glint in her eyes.

That was enough to stop Steve's grumbling. "Nope. That's just fine. No worries. We are happy to wait for Mia to get better control," the gargoyles both scrambled to say.

Vivi winked at Mia. The gesture made Mia smile, confirming that the offer wasn't genuine, or even a way to torment the gargoyles more, but a way to back Mia up. It made the red-haired halfling reflect on the continued changes in Vivi. She was constantly growing, and Mia was happy to see how she was turning out.

As Vivi walked away, Zander sidled up to Mia. "What's going on with Vivi recently? Why is she becoming such a team player?"

Mia shrugged. "I don't know, but I'm happy about it."

Zander smiled as they went to the portal that would take them to Scotland. When they walked through, he turned to her again. "Um, I wanted to know if…I mean, later, well, if you're hungry, would you like to have dinner?" he asked.

Mia looked at him strangely. "Of course, we can all have dinner. There's a little restaurant we didn't get to try last time."

"Oh, yeah. That sounds great. But I was just thinking…I mean, not all of us," Zander tried again.

"Very smooth, Zander," Carson teased. "At this rate, you should be able to get a date with her by the time we graduate… from college."

Mia realized what was happening and blushed. She glanced away, then looked back at Zander and nodded. "I'd love to have dinner with you," she said with a smile.

CHAPTER TWENTY-SIX

Mia spent the day looking forward to dinner. She went back and forth between being excited to spend time with Zander, and anxious that it was officially an actual date. It was different from the other times they had spent alone together. They would often receive curious looks from their friends, and from other students who saw them.

And Mia had always felt that the time she spent with Zander was special, more than if it was any of her other friends. But she and Zander had never talked about it. They had never confirmed they were anything more than just friends. This time was different. This time he had purposely asked her out on a date, and she was eager to see how that change was going to feel.

As the end of the day grew closer, Mia wished she had the chance to change clothes before dinner. It didn't feel as much like a date when she was going in what she had worn all day. But when it was finally time to leave, one smile from Zander made her not care what she was wearing. He looked so happy to see her that she couldn't wait for them to go off together.

If only they could actually be alone.

"Where do you want to go for dinner?" Alania asked as they

walked away.

Zander and Mia turned and looked at her questioningly.

"We're going to dinner together," Zander said.

The faerie looked at him for a few seconds, as though waiting for him to remember something. When he didn't say anything else, she put one little hand to her chest.

"I'm your chaperone, remember? The other guardians and I were assigned to be with the five of you while you are not on campus. You two aren't allowed to go off by yourself together. I have to be with you. Elmhurst was very clear that you can't be without us," she told them.

Zander and Mia exchanged a disappointed look. Neither had thought of the restrictions when they made the date earlier, and they weren't looking forward to having the entire group tag along with them. But they also knew there was no way Elmhurst would give them any special consideration on their need for a chaperone simply to go to dinner together. They agreed and went to the small restaurant Mia had thought would be romantic. Which now seemed nothing but cramped.

The hostess guided Zander and Mia to their own table, but the rest of the group were seated a few feet away. It didn't give them any real privacy, and every few seconds Mia or Zander would look at the other table and see one of the halflings peeking at them or whispering as they stared.

What had begun as something they were both looking forward to, quickly turned into an awkward situation. They barely spoke, and instead gazed around the restaurant, and occasionally smiled at each other uncomfortably.

"Was your dinner good?" Zander asked after they finished their almost silent meal.

"It was delicious. Thank you. Did you enjoy yours?"

Zander nodded. "I've never seen a restaurant attempt a vegan Scotch Egg. That's hard to do when the entire dish is just a hard-boiled egg wrapped in sausage."

Mia laughed. "But it tasted good?"

"It really did. They managed to make the tofu in the center taste like an egg."

The waitress strolled up to the edge of the table and asked if they wanted dessert. They both said they did, and she handed them menus, waiting the few seconds it took for them to decide on lemon sorbet with raspberries.

When she walked away, Zander put his hands on the table. One twitched as though he was thinking about reaching for her hand. Mia wanted him to, but the others being so close stopped him. Alania fluttered past as though she was going to the restroom, but she was eyeing them, making it obvious she was checking in.

Mia wished they could be alone, even for a short time. A second later, the restaurant around them disappeared. They popped up on a distant part of the island at the edge of a cliff, still sitting at their table from the restaurant. Ahead of them, the Sea of Hebrides rolled and crashed against the rocks. It was beautiful, and Mia knew exactly what had happened. Her wish had been enough to accidentally create a portal that sucked them through it and away from the others right to this spot.

Several yards away, Alania kept her distance from the couple. When the portal had appeared, she had been close enough to get sucked through with them. At first, she was shocked, but she remembered what Cinder had told her about Mia and her skills.

She couldn't really be aggravated about it. She knew of Mia's abilities, and the portal appearing that way only meant the halfling had deeply wanted the time with Zander. Besides, they were still on the island, and they were in a safe place. Cinder and two other faerie guardians were with the other three, so Alania decided to give them a few moments to themselves. It was cute watching them together, and she knew when the time came, she would easily create a portal to bring them back.

The only problem would be if humans saw the creation of the

portal in the restaurant. But she'd deal with that when they returned.

The sky was clear, and the moon was bright enough in the darkness for Zander and Mia to see each other clearly. Happy to be alone with Mia no matter what the circumstance, Zander stood from the table and walked around to Mia. He finally took her hand in his, pulling her up to stand next to him.

"It's a good thing Dan and Steve aren't here with us. They would have told Elmhurst on us for sure," he said.

"They really don't seem to be able to keep a secret from her," Mia agreed.

They laughed, and Zander brushed his fingers along the side of her face. He leaned in to kiss her. Just before their lips touched, they tumbled backward through a portal that formed directly behind them. They landed in a heap at Cassia's feet, and when they looked around, they saw the rest of the Scooby Gang gathered nearby.

Cassia glared at them angrily. "What do you think you're doing?"

Alania moved forward to defend them. "I was with them the entire time, and they were safe."

"It doesn't matter. Mia shouldn't be creating portals. She knows the rules, and how dangerous it could be for her to just travel around on a whim," Cassia argued.

"How did you know where we were?" Mia asked. "Or that I created the portal that got us there?"

"I will always know when you are in trouble," Cassia replied.

It wasn't really an answer, but the cryptic message made Mia stay silent.

"That's not exactly true. You didn't know we were in the Louvre until after the fact," Carson quipped.

Cassia turned an angry scowl on him, and Luna tugged him back by his elbow.

"You aren't helping matters," Luna said.

"I didn't create the portal on purpose," Mia insisted. "It just sort of appeared. It's not like I asked for it."

Cassia turned to Alania. "Where did they go?"

"Just to the cliffs across the island," the faerie told her.

Cassia nodded, her expression relaxing slightly. "Well, at least you didn't go too far. I'm glad for that. But you better not do it again. Do you understand me?"

"I didn't do it on purpose," Mia said again, her voice growing louder and higher with frustration.

"Are you going to rat on her to Elmhurst?" Luna asked.

The other halflings looked at her in surprise, shocked Luna would ask something like that.

Cassia seemed to think about the options for a few seconds, then finally shook her head. "No. Mia insists she didn't do it on purpose—"

"I didn't!"

"And as I was going to say, I believe her. And since Alania was along, and no one was hurt, I don't see the need," Cassia finished.

Mia nodded in acknowledgment, but couldn't bring herself to thank Cassia. She didn't feel like she had done anything wrong, and it would have been needlessly harsh of her guardian to report her to the headmistress for something she hadn't intended to do.

"Good. Can we get back to our food now?" Carson asked. "I'm really looking forward to dessert."

Cassia nodded and turned to leave. She took a few steps, then paused and looked over her shoulder at Zander and Mia. "He is pretty cute," she said and winked at Mia.

Carson, Vivi, Luna, and the faeries, burst into laughter as Zander and Mia hung their heads in embarrassment, their cheeks flushing. This wasn't the way they had expected their first date would go. But at least they'd had those few seconds together, and they weren't in trouble.

CHAPTER TWENTY-SEVEN

In the shadows outside the restaurant, hiding in an alley between the building and the bicycle shop next door, stood a short, squat figure, watching the door intently. Beady eyes scanned the street over and over as it waited for the target to exit. Every time the door opened, the bogan would prepare to follow her, to isolate her, but each time it was someone else.

Growing tired of the wait, his rat-like nose twitched. He stroked his long beard and pulled his long brown cape around himself. The night was getting cold, and though the temperature didn't necessarily bother the bogan if he kept moving, standing still presented a bit more of a challenge. Sitting still too long for a bogan was a boredom that could barely be withstood.

The bogan hopped from one foot to the other to keep himself entertained and watched as the door opened once again, and a fae creature stepped outside. This excited him because he knew this particular creature. It was the one they called Cassia, and she was here with the target. If she was leaving, it was either with his assignment, or she was leaving it unprotected. Either scenario satisfied him.

Cassia stepped out into the night and instinctively knew

something was up. Keeping her cool, she took a few steps, allowing her senses to take control, and finding herself drawn to a dark corner in an alley beside the building. Something was there, though she couldn't be sure what, and she had to find somewhere to observe it. It came as no surprise that things would be following Mia, especially now, and especially here in Scotland, where there were so many creatures.

Cassia didn't let on that anything was wrong, and went down the sidewalk, away from the restaurant and rounded a corner. As soon as she was past it, and out of sight, she pulled a small makeup mirror, opened it, aiming it behind her and around the building.

She angled it at the shadowy corner and watched as first, a nose poked out from the darkness, followed by the head. She exhaled in relief when she figured out it was just a bogan. As ugly and mischievous as they were, they often weren't capable of much violence, and with the faeries inside with the kids, she was confident that an army of bogans would be no match for them. Not with someone as powerful as Mia was becoming, at any rate.

Something ahead of her drew her attention off the bogan, and she slammed the mirror closed. The thing she saw was unmistakable and far more dangerous than a mere bogan. It crept down another alley, away from the restaurant on the next street, hunting something.

Whatever it was hunting was in danger, and since it was a redcap, its victim was likely a child. One last time, Cassia glanced around the corner at the alley where the bogan was hiding and sprinted toward the redcap.

She stopped at the corner of the alley the redcap had entered and popped her head around it. The alley was dark, though not pitch black. A lone light shone over a door near the end of the alley, above a fire-exit for one of the buildings.

In the distance, between the redcap and the light, was a small child, no more than eight years old, lost, scared, and running.

Suddenly the redcap stopped sneaking and hauled off after the child, its mouth opening wide, saliva trailing on the ground behind it.

Cassia burst into a run, pushing herself to make it to the redcap before it did any damage. Its wiry arms reached out, and its long brown beard flowed behind it. She heard the cry of the child as the redcap's hands grabbed him, pulling him closer.

The child tried to scream, but nothing came out as the image of such a horrible creature struck him so full of fear that all sound refused to leave his throat. Terrified, he struggled against the grip of the redcap as its long fingernails dug painfully into his arms, and he lost control of his bladder. His face was disappearing inside the terrible creature's mouth, and soon all the child could see was the horrible sharp teeth, dripping with wet, sticky spit.

With a crack, Cassia's foot connected with the side of the redcap's head, forcing the neck to snap to the side. Its hands opened, releasing the child. The boy tumbled to the ground and rolled to safety in a dark corner.

He pulled a trash can lid close to him like a shield, watching as Cassia landed gracefully on her feet and charged after the thing on the ground. It hopped up on its feet and spun into a kick that landed hard in her stomach. She doubled over and stumbled into the wall of the alley.

The redcap dove at her, gnashing its terrible teeth and swinging its nails at her like blades. She recovered in time to knock the hands away and shove her elbow into its jaw. A punch to its nose sent it backward, and she leaned into a thrust-kick that sent it barreling backward against the other wall.

A flurry of punches to its side weakened the redcap, and she knew she was gaining the upper hand. Cassia was pulling her arm back for a knockout blow when she was suddenly stopped by a cry from the boy in the shadows.

He was peering over the trashcan lid, his eyes wide and terrified, and his mouth open in a full scream. The terror locking up his voice before it could be released, and now he was wailing for help and for his mother. It was mostly unintelligible cries, but the cry for his mother was piercing and loud, and Cassia felt for him.

With her attention diverted for a split second too long, the redcap escaped her grip. It started to run for freedom to the open end of the alley, and she dove after it, barely grasping its leg with her hand.

"Let go," the thing hissed and kicked at her.

"Not a chance." Cassia yanked the leg back toward her, grabbing at the foot to put it in an ankle lock.

The redcap rolled with the momentum, swung its other foot into her jaw, knocking her loose, and making purple spots appear on the edge of her vision. She grasped again for the thing, but missed and, though still woozy, had to get to her feet to chase it. The screams of the child were echoing through the alley as she grabbed the redcap just before he pulled free. Cassia tugged him into a headlock. He struggled against her and then bit her forearm hard. She screamed in pain.

"Stop biting me!" she shouted to no avail. It gnawed at her, trying to bite through the thick leather she wore, and undoubtedly would try to eat her arm clean off in an effort to escape.

Cassia had to think fast, and the sounds of feet pounding on the sidewalk outside the alley meant someone was coming to help the child. But worse, it meant they would see both her and the redcap. She focused as fast as she could, opened a portal to Forasaon against the wall of the building, and yanked on the redcap's head to shove it toward the prison. It tried to fight her, but she dragged it a few feet closer. If she could get him through, she could take him to prison, and allow her to get back to keeping an eye on Mia.

It sank its nails into her sides and thrashed wildly in her grip, but she was too strong. She could feel blood beginning to slide down her sides as the creature dug into her, desperate not to go through the portal.

Voices were coming from outside the alley, meaning she only had seconds. She lurched with the redcap in her arm, popped her hip to one side, and threw herself and the creature through the portal and into darkness.

CHAPTER TWENTY-EIGHT

Usually, Cassia's arrivals at the prison were smooth and controlled. She moved through portals as though walking through a door, and could easily enter the prison without bringing much attention to herself. Not so this time. Rather than guiding herself through the portal with ease, and walking comfortably into the prison, she tumbled through like a child learning to create their first portal.

The pair flailed and fell through, and the redcap wrenched himself free of Cassia's hand. The instant they hit the ground in the prison, he got to his feet and tried to flee. One of the ogres standing guard laughed when he saw the redcap, and he reached for it. Cassia watched the ogre snatch the redcap by the scruff of his collar, and pick him up as if he was nothing more than a stray cat getting in the way.

"Well, that was quite the entrance," Fan said, laughing. "What is going on here? Cassia, I've never seen you go through a portal like that. What happened?"

Cassia sighed, exasperated as she waved his words off, and got to her feet. She pointed angrily at the redcap. "This creature was caught trying to eat a small boy in Scotland during the games."

The amusement disappeared from Fan's eyes, and his expression turned serious. He released a sigh that said he was very unhappy to hear about the incident. "That's really too bad. The Fae Council put out an edict ahead of the games this year. Anyone caught messing with the humans in Scotland during the games is to immediately get the ax."

"She's lying," the redcap cried, trying to lunge for Fan in desperation. "I would never try to eat a child!"

"I saw you," Cassia insisted.

"That's preposterous. A child is far too easy prey. No self-respecting redcap would bother with kids, especially not when there were so many halflings around that would taste so much better," the redcap said, his pleading fading to mocking as his mouth curled into a grotesque smile.

Fan scoffed and looked at the ogre, still holding the redcap. "See that it's done."

"On it," the ogre said, dragging the redcap away.

Fan turned to Cassia with a smirk. "I guess you'll be wanting the bounty for that one?"

Cassia nodded. "If there is a bounty, I want it. I got him here. Maybe not in the smoothest way I've ever brought somebody in, but I got him here, and the kid didn't get turned into a midnight snack. I think that warrants the reward."

"I agree, and as it turns out, there is a bounty on his head. He was telling the truth, though. This redcap is not in the habit of going after little kids. Not to say the games didn't inspire him to try something new and go for a quick refreshment in the form of a kid, but that's not his usual thing. He tends to favor the halflings. Which means the bounty isn't too high."

"Halfling murderers don't bring in high bounties anymore?" Cassia asked. "Nobody's worried about the halflings?"

"Not as much during the games. The Fae Council is putting a lot more attention on the humans right now. They are much more worried about them," Fan answered.

"Why? What's going on?" Cassia asked.

"There has been a lot of activity in the human realm lately, and they are worried the humans are going to catch on soon. Too many of them are beginning to see things they shouldn't and are asking too many questions," Fan explained.

That wasn't what Cassia wanted to hear. She was already worried enough about Mia. Now this news merely put more pressure on her. "Great," she said. "That's all I need. More humans learning the truth and forming their own bounty-hunter parties."

Her frustration was obvious as she planted her hands on her hips and paced across the dimly lit chamber. Human interaction with the fae world was almost never a good thing. Of course, there were exceptions.

The locals on the Isle of Raasay who served the fae and ensured events happened smoothly were very helpful. Humans working in the corporations and in conjunction with fae also helped to protect the fae and the security of their world.

But these were very limited exceptions. Most of the time, when humans interacted with the fae, it created serious problems that had ripple effects for the entire world. The worst were the ones who thought they were helping by going after criminals. All too often, they ended up in danger, or they hurt innocent fae.

"Speaking of bounty hunters, the Fae Council wants to bump up efforts to limit the criminal activity, and reduce the danger for the humans who are around. There are so many more criminals here because of the games, and the Council wants to make sure there aren't any issues with multiple deaths, or with humans making connections with the criminals," Fan said.

"That sounds like a fun adventure," Cassia said sarcastically.

"It's good to hear you say that," Fan said, deciding to skip over her sarcasm and pretend she was being sincere. "It just so happens you stumbled into my neck of the woods right at the perfect time. I was about to call you with a special assignment."

That didn't sound appealing to Cassia. She shook her head. "Nope, not happening," she said.

"You didn't even hear what the special assignment was. How are you going to refuse to help?" Fan asked.

"It doesn't matter what it is. I'm not doing it. I'm helping the Elmhurst Academy right now, and trust me, there is plenty for me to be doing there. I don't need to stack anything else on top of it. It's all I can do to make sure they have the extra protection they need with the games going on," Cassia told him.

The jailer stared at her, his expression stern and unchanging. She knew what he was thinking. "You know the council doesn't care much for halflings," he said darkly.

Cassia stiffened at the sentiment. She'd always had a problem with the way the fae council looked at halflings, and with the prejudiced manner in which they handled protecting or defending them. It was worse now that she had Mia in her life. She hated the thought of Mia being overlooked or mistreated, simply because of her halfling parentage.

"I know," she said flatly. "That's why I'm helping the academy. The Council doesn't care to. The way they see the halflings, and how little they seem to care about them is baffling. Some of them have their own halfling children. They should be worried."

Cassia and Fan looked at each other. Behind them, the ogre guard who had remained struggled to hold back a laugh. Cassia's lips tingled. Fan was fighting his own laugh. Finally, they gave in, and both broke into a cascade of laughter.

"The Council? Worried?" the ogre said through his laughs. "About their own children? Listen close, and you might be able to hear the redcaps in hell strapping on their skis."

This made Fan laugh harder. "If the members of the Fae Council ever actually started caring about their own halfling children, I think it would be too cold in hell to even go skiing," he said.

"They'd all be frozen solid," Cassia agreed.

They all knew the Fae Council couldn't care less about their own halfling children. Most of them wouldn't even acknowledge they existed. They were the result of flings with humans and were simply cast aside. Many never met their halfling children, and those who did barely behaved like the kids were alive, much less like they mattered to them at all.

If the Council didn't care about their own children because they were halflings, nothing was going to make a whole academy full of unrelated halflings mean anything to them.

CHAPTER TWENTY-NINE

The restaurant where the kids were eating, along with Cinder and Alania, was in an area where humans were quite used to seeing fae. However, that didn't stop Sam from crying out in surprise when the flame from the match lighting his cigarette illuminated the bogan a few feet away. He released another short, high-pitched cry as the bogan slammed his head into the wall, knocking him unconscious. It had a plan, and it needed the body alive.

The bogan stood over the fallen waiter and cast the spell to take the waiter's form, using it as a glamour. It would be a convincing glamour, one that would allow him to move through the restaurant. He was glad it only needed the illusion to last for a very short amount of time. This man wasn't something he wanted to look like for long. The creature opened the door to the back of the restaurant and kicked aside the wooden block holding it open, in case the waiter regained consciousness and tried to come inside to warn people.

The kitchen was chaotic. The games provided a huge surge of business and kept the cooks and servers hopping almost from the minute they opened until closing very early in the morning. This would help to keep the bogan under the radar. Most of the young people in the restaurant wouldn't see through the glamour, but the full fae would if they looked long enough. The busy atmosphere would make it easier for him to blend in and go unnoticed.

It didn't take as long as he had expected. Within moments of stepping into the dining room, the bogan saw the perfect opportunity to fulfill his mission. His eyes locked on a waitress carrying a tray of fragile glasses. She was balancing far too many of them to remain steady if she happened to trip on something. And she was heading directly for the girl the bogan had been told to target. He needed blood, and shattered glass was great for that.

The bogan crossed the room and placed himself between the oncoming waitress and the table of kids. At the right moment, he stuck out a foot, tripping the woman. It wasn't elegant, but it worked. Glasses tumbled and crashed into the halflings' table, shattering on impact. The bogan, not leaving anything to chance, snatched a shard and feigned a stumble backward into Mia, aiming at her hand in the chaos.

"What the heck," Zander exclaimed as he jumped up, wine now drenching his shirt.

"Oh, I'm so sorry," the waitress stammered. "Let me get something to help you clean up."

"You're bleeding," the bogan told Mia, feigning shock. "Here, put this on it until she gets back." He handed her a white cloth, which she put over the wound to soak up the small stream of blood.

Mia inspected the cut. "Thanks. It's not bad, actually. Just a little slice. My shirt is ruined, though," she said, looking down at the giant green stain from something sticky that had landed on her in the fall.

The waitress returned quickly with napkins and a first-aid kit. As soon as the bandages were brought out, Mia dropped the white cloth, and the bogan picked it up, stuffing it in his pocket as he shoveled glass into a dustpan. He walked away, snickering at how easy it had been. He tossed the entire dustpan in the trash and headed for the back door. No one saw a thing.

Or so he thought.

Inside the restaurant, Alania pursed her lips. The waitress tripping as she walked by Mia could have been an accident. Things like that happened all the time in restaurants, especially when they were as busy as this one. But she couldn't help but notice when the waiter took the cloth stained with Mia's blood and slipped it into his pocket as he walked by. There was something strange about him. She watched him hurry across the room and saw the tell-tale shimmer around him.

She fluttered up from her place at the table and motioned for Lily to join her. "I think that waiter was actually a glamour. Go follow him," she said, pointing to the kitchen door. Lily nodded and took off without a word.

"We should get back to campus," Carson said. "I know you don't think the cut is that bad, but you should still see the campus nurse. Last thing we want is Elmhurst getting upset that we didn't follow protocol again."

"Carson's right," Zander said. "Besides, I need to get out of this shirt. I smell like alcohol, and I can only guess what Elmhurst would say about that."

The owner of the restaurant waved them off when they asked for the check, insisting that the whole incident was reason enough to comp the meal, and the Five went to the portal to campus. Most of the gang returned to their rooms for the night, but Luna, Alania, Cinder, and Mia, went to the nurse for Mia's cut.

A few hours later, Mia was settled in her room, and Cinder accompanied Alania back to the lounge on the bottom floor. Most of the students were already gone, leaving the two faeries alone in a corner by the fire.

Cinder scooted close to Alania and whispered, "What's going on? You've barely said a word since we got back."

"Someone used a glamour to cut Mia on purpose," Alania said flatly.

"What? It was an accident. She was cut by glass," Cinder argued.

"No, she wasn't. I think it was a bogan. I can't be sure, though. I sent Lily to check it out," Alania explained.

"Speaking of," Cinder said, glancing over Alania's shoulder. "Here she comes."

Alania rose to greet her, and Lily sat next to Cinder. She seemed upset, which Cinder took to mean bad news. "What did you find out?" Alania said, not wasting any time.

"Yeah, tell us what happened," said Cinder. In spite of the worrisome charge Alania had just mentioned, she was excited to be working with her cousin on something that might be important.

"Well, it was definitely a bogan."

"Knew it," Alania said under her breath, shaking her head.

"Yeah, he had cast a glamour of some poor waiter who was knocked out outside in the alley," Lily said. "I checked to make sure he was alive, but he looked like he got his clock cleaned pretty good. Then I noticed a bogan running away from the restaurant with the white cloth the waiter had in his pocket. So, I followed him around the corner and through a portal."

"And?" Cinder asked.

"It's not good."

"How not good?" Alania asked.

"When I came out, I saw him go into a house. I stayed around in the shadows a while until I noticed a light on in his basement. He has a lab down there, and he was doing something with the cloth. It looked like he was testing it. For what I don't know."

"DNA," Alania shrieked. "He got her DNA. Crickets!"

"What should I do now?" Lily asked.

Alania thought for a moment before answering. There were a lot of moving parts now, and things had to be done in a certain way to keep everyone safe. "Go back to Guardian Myla and tell her what you told me. Now. Quickly."

Lily nodded, and left immediately, leaving Alania and Cinder alone once again. Cinder was fuming, but Alania was trying to keep calm.

"We should tell Mia," Cinder said. "She deserves to know."

"We can't. Not yet," Alania insisted.

"Why? She might be in terrible danger, and she deserves to know she might need to look over her shoulder."

"*We're* supposed to be looking over her shoulder. That's our job. And tonight, we failed, and let a bogan get her blood. If she knew, who knows what she would try to do. She might do something stupid, and we wouldn't be able to help her. If she is who we think she is, we need to keep her safe at all costs, including not letting her know what she doesn't need to know yet."

"Cassia. We should tell Cassia then," Cinder said, frustrated. "She's the girl's protector and fae guardian. If no one else, *she* needs to know."

Alania took this under consideration for a moment. Despite the embarrassment of having allowed something to happen to Mia, she knew Cassia was the best person to handle the information, and she definitely needed to know. She nodded.

"Tomorrow. When we see her tomorrow, we will tell her. But for now, we should go back to the dorm room, and try to get some rest."

CHAPTER THIRTY

ia had expected Cassia to be there when she got up the
next day. The bounty hunter had been so angry and
worried that Mia was all but positive she was going to wake up to
her guardian sitting there in her room, making sure she was
where she was supposed to be.

When no Cassia appeared, Mia couldn't help but feel relieved.
Her guardian must be on assignment somewhere and didn't have
the time to come check in on her. Or ask her a bunch of embarrassing questions about her date with Zander. Not having Cassia
there to bug her or spy on her was exactly what she needed.

Down at breakfast, Cinder was worried, too. "You were
supposed to be watching her," she hissed at Alania. "You were
given an important responsibility. Don't you understand that?"

"Of course, I understand that. I might be younger than you,
but that doesn't mean I'm stupid. I know what I'm supposed to be
doing," Alania retorted.

"Then why aren't you doing it? You were right there, and look
what happened!"

"It was just an accident. Nobody knew that was going to
happen."

"Do you have any idea what could happen if there's another accident like that again?" Cinder asked. Cinder had stewed all night over the incident, and how they had allowed the bogan to get away with Mia's DNA. She was as angry as a dragon whose lair had been raided. If she could control her fire, she'd probably spit fire at that bogan right then and there.

Zander overheard the conversation between the faeries and moved along the table toward them. "What's going on?" he asked.

Cinder looked at him and promptly sneezed. The spark hit the hem of Zander's shirt and set the fabric on fire. He swatted at it a few times, hopping up from his seat to shake the shirt and make the flames die down. It only took a few seconds for the fire to go out, but he glared at the little faerie, frustrated that she couldn't control her sneezes better.

"Don't aim at me next time," he said. He looked at the damage to his shirt and released an exasperated sigh. "Great. Now I'm going to have to go back to the dorm and change shirts before I can go to class. I guess there won't be any breakfast for me today."

He stormed off, and Cinder watched him for a few seconds before turning back to Alania. That was what she had intended to happen. She needed him to leave the conversation and not overhear more. Hopefully, the brief little fire would quickly leave his mind, and he wouldn't hold it against her.

That didn't work out. Cinder didn't see him again until later in the day after all his classes were over. She smiled at him pleasantly, but he stalked to her with a glare.

"Cinder, what is going on?" he demanded.

She widened her eyes and looked at him with the most innocent expression she could manage. "What? What are you talking about? Did something happen?"

Zander wasn't impressed. He knew something was up, and he wasn't going to let her off the hook no matter how cute she tried to be. "Don't try that with me. I know something's going on, and you need to tell me what it is. I can't help protect Mia if I don't know what I'm supposed to be protecting her from. I need all the information," he said.

Alania shook her head, but Cinder knew she wasn't going to get by with any more diversion. "Mia is in danger," Cinder said.

"I already know that," he said. "That's why everyone needs to be working together to protect her as much as we can."

"It's a lot more than you and the others know," she added.

Alania shook her head again, pressing her lips together to stop herself from saying anything. She swatted at her cousin, trying to make her be quiet.

"What do you mean?" Zander asked.

"Shhhh," Alania said harshly, trying to keep Cinder from going any further without saying anything herself.

"No," Cinder said, shaking her head. "I'm done. I'm tired of keeping secrets, and I don't want to do it anymore. If there's anyone who is going to be able to help Mia, it's Zander. He cares about her and won't let her get hurt. But he has to know what's really going on if he's going to be able to help her."

Zander's worry immediately skyrocketed. His eyes snapped back and forth between the faeries and finally landed on Alania. "If you don't stop trying to keep secrets about Mia from me, I will glue your wings together," he threatened.

This ticked the little faerie off. She was trying to do her job and didn't appreciate him being so aggressive with her. She wriggled a little closer and sneezed on him. Zander was accustomed to Cinder sneezing and lighting things on fire, but he wasn't prepared for Alania's sneezing abilities.

As soon as the little faerie sneezed in his direction, Zander's feet left the ground, and he was floating in the air. With a single flick of her hand, ropes appeared out of nowhere. The long lengths wrapped around Zander, tying him up so he wasn't able to move. He struggled against them, trying to escape, but it was of no use.

"You're not going to get out of those ropes," Alania told him. "They were made out of the vines around the faerie pools. They were enchanted specifically to hold fae in place. You can't get out of them."

"Alania doesn't like to be insulted," Cinder said.

"I'm sorry," Zander said. He gritted his teeth to prevent any more words from coming out. He was smart enough to keep quiet while she still had him subdued and floating around in the air.

"Listen to me carefully. I am the guardian. I will be the one protecting the princess, not you," Alania said firmly.

Zander's eyes widened, and his mouth fell open, but he stopped himself before he said anything. However, in his silence, he swore he would do anything he had to in order to protect Mia.

What Alania had said was the confirmation he needed. He knew for sure now that Mia was the missing heir. They had all suspected that she was. As soon as they started learning more about Princess Violet, they had come to the conclusion that Mia must be descended from her. But Princess Violet died almost two thousand years ago. At least, that was what everyone assumed. That meant Mia couldn't be very closely related to her, and why they had all said she couldn't be related. But Zander knew everyone, well, everyone except for Vivi, still considered it a possibility.

The human blood that made her a halfling only tainted her lineage further. It complicated things. Mia had already said she didn't want to claim her heritage, which meant no one should be worried about her. That would be the only reason anyone should want to be after her. But it was obvious someone was concerned about the possibility of her deciding she wanted to claim her right to the throne.

Even though she had too much human blood in her to truly take the throne, someone was upset by the possibility, enough to want to kill her. He was extremely confused by it all, but that didn't do anything to change how he felt. He still wanted to do anything he could to protect her.

"I care about Mia very much," he finally said to Alania. "I would do anything to protect her, and would never want anything to happen to her."

The faerie flew up to look him straight in the eye. She pointed at him firmly. "I am swearing you to absolute secrecy. You can't say anything about any of this to anyone," she said.

"I won't," he promised.

"Not even Mia. She doesn't need to be worried about it all," she added.

Zander nodded his agreement, and Alania let him float back to the ground. The rope disappeared in a sudden poof. He hurried away from them, wanting to find Mia as much as he wanted to be away from them.

As soon as he was gone, Cinder looked at her cousin. "He already suspected her lineage. We found out last semester that she is most likely a descendant of Princess Violet, but very far down the line. It has been too long since her death for them to be closely related," she said.

"Suspecting is one thing. Knowing is another," Alania said. "He needs to keep his mouth shut."

Around the corner, Vivi leaned against the building, listening to the conversation. She had watched the entire interaction with Zander, and now her eyes sparkled with an evil glint. She gathered her books and rushed off to the dorm, where she knew she would find Mia.

CHAPTER THIRTY-ONE

Vivi returned to the dorm room, and burst inside, eager to tell Mia what she had heard so she could watch her reaction. But when she entered, she saw Elmhurst had arrived. Luna and Mia were both sitting on the edge of Luna's bed, and they turned to look at Vivi when she came in.

"Is everything all right?" Vivi asked.

Having the headmistress in their room wasn't something that happened often. She highly doubted Elmhurst would just come by to say hello and check in on them. Something had to have brought her to see them.

"I was just telling them that Cassia has been called away on Council business," Elmhurst said.

Vivi nodded as she went to her bed. She decided to keep what she had heard to herself, at least for now. As much as she had wanted to be the one to tell Mia, and to be there to see her response, she wasn't going to do it while Elmhurst was standing there. She didn't want the headmistress to know and take drastic actions.

As upset as Vivi had been when they had first learned they had to take Mia into their group, she had since seen the benefits.

In the short time they had worked together, the group had managed to achieve the Power of Five on several occasions and were growing stronger. They would be able to do so much more as time went on. It would help all of them accomplish their goals, and put Vivi in a stronger position to earn the accolades and attention from the prestigious schools and roles she wanted to attract.

She didn't want the headmistress to take Mia away. Not yet, anyway. Maybe after graduation, but that thought made her pause. If they kept working together after graduation, they could achieve more. Suddenly, it hit Vivi. Did she really want to keep Mia around? She could barely believe it herself.

"Oh, and Vivi," Elmhurst said a few moments later. Vivi looked up from folding the clothes she had dug through that morning to choose her outfit as she contemplated what to do with her juicy news. Elmhurst was holding a piece of paper out to her. "This came in from your father earlier. He asked that I give it to you."

The sound of the principal's voice didn't give Vivi a lot of hope that the message contained in the note was a good one. She took it and sat on her bed, holding the folded paper in her lap while the headmistress said her goodbyes and left. When she was gone, Vivi opened the note and stared down at it.

"Are you okay?" Luna asked several seconds later when Vivi hadn't looked up from the paper again.

"What does it say?" Mia asked.

Vivi shook her head and balled up the paper. She hopped off the bed and left the room without answering. This was something she didn't want to tell them. Her father had yet again canceled plans with her. This time they had arranged to attend a game together.

He had told her to return the ticket he had bought for her to attend the major league game that upcoming weekend. Instead of going with her, he was planning to use her ticket to schmooze a fae who had offices in Europe. It was an important business contract, he explained, as though that was all she needed to hear to be understanding. It was an important business contract, so the promise he had made to his daughter didn't matter. It was expected that she should accept and be fine with it.

At least he had given some sort of concession to the idea of her feelings. According to him, since both of the Slamball Major League teams competing at the event on Saturday were from Europe, he figured she wouldn't care about seeing them. Using the tickets for his European business contact would be a more advantageous use of it.

Of course, that didn't matter to her. She didn't care why he believed the ticket would be better used by someone else. She only cared that he had given it to her and had planned on seeing a game with her, then he had gone back on his word. As usual.

She was hurt, and seriously ticked off. There was a time when her initial reaction would have been to put someone else down or cause problems for someone else, likely Mia. This time, instead of being a bully, she decided to make herself feel better by going out and having fun. That's why she was on her way to find Carson. He would be up for anything.

She was right that he would be up for some fun, but it wasn't going to be just the two of them. After she explained what had happened, Carson pointed out that it would do her good to be around the entire group.

No matter what she said or what she wanted people to think, she got a lot of comfort and support from the five. They worked hard together, but they also managed to have a lot of fun. Vivi reluctantly agreed, and they made plans to go into Edinburgh and sightsee, foregoing anything to do with Slamball, and instead, experiencing new things, and having fun together.

———

In his hidden lair, Narco was far from having fun. The test result came back on the blood the bogan had managed to harvest from Mia, but it was confusing. The blood had ruined the test, leaving a mess instead of true results. He realized by looking at it that even her blood had been touched by the spell meant to keep prying eyes away from the girl's genetic secrets. He was furious.

At this rate, he wouldn't have anything to compare to the royal DNA, should he even be able to get a sample from his shadow contact. Without a clean DNA strand from the girl, Narco's contact wouldn't attempt to get something from one of the queens.

"Try again," Narco demanded. "Obviously there's something wrong with the test. You have to try again. You said blood wouldn't be impacted by a spell."

Orin shook his head. "Trying again won't do any good, Narco. The same thing would happen. It is extremely rare, and only someone of the highest levels of power can do it, but some are capable of putting a genetic cloaking-spell on blood. I told you that you would need some of Mia's blood if you wanted to test her because I didn't think she would be affected by that kind of enchantment. I've never seen it myself."

"Then how could it have happened? If it is so rare, how could this be?" Narco asked.

"Princess Violet must have cast a generational spell," Orin suggested.

"Generational spells are from ancient times. Even before Princess Violet," Narco pointed out. "Fae haven't messed with them in a long time."

"She must have learned the details of it before she left the fae realm. Perhaps she took a book or two of ancient spells with her and learned about it from them. I've heard that some ancient texts went missing when the kingdom split. She must have wanted to mask herself and any offspring she had," Orin told him.

Narco shook his head, not convinced by the idea. "I can't believe it would still be in effect all these years later. It's been over two millennia, for crickets' sake!"

"Rumor has it, the third princess was just as powerful as her two sisters," Orin told him.

Narco thought about Queen Mab and her incredible power, then about Queen Tatiana and how powerful she was. He scowled.

"Mia can't be as powerful as Mab and Tatiana. She's a halfling. It's just not possible. There has to be a way to remove the spell protecting her DNA," he said.

Orin nodded, relenting to his associate's intense refusals. "Fine. I will work on it. But we'll need more blood. We don't have enough left to run an effective test," he said.

"That's not a problem," Narco agreed. "I could send a redcap in to get at least a finger."

Orin shook his head firmly. "No. That will cause too much attention. She's already been injured. I will send another associate to the school to get her bandages. There will be enough within the bandages to work on the spell. Then once I've figured that out, if we need more, we can contemplate doing something more severe."

"All right," Narco said. "But we need to move quickly. There isn't any time to spare. We need her DNA."

CHAPTER THIRTY-TWO

"Do you think we stayed in our dorm rooms long enough to qualify as having slept here?" Luna asked as the group gathered together in the predawn darkness.

It was four in the morning on Saturday, and they were getting an early start to make sure they could fit as much in their day as they possibly could before having to obey the curfew Elmhurst had set. With Scotland so many hours ahead of them, starting this early in the morning meant they had already missed a few hours of the day there. The group didn't want to miss anything else.

"We were in our rooms, weren't we?" Carson asked. "And we definitely slept after midnight."

"And Elmhurst didn't say anything about how long we had to be in bed. She didn't make any specifications about leaving before the crack of dawn. Just that we had to be in our rooms, and sleep in our beds," Vivi said.

"I'm really not interested in any more arguments about technicalities," Luna said. "That run-in with Elmhurst was enough for me."

"It's not a technicality," Zander reassured her. "It is morning."

"And think about it," Mia added. "We've gotten this early of a start before, like on days when we were practicing our spells. There were times when we left even earlier than this, and she never said anything about it."

"That's true," Luna said.

"Great," Vivi said. "I already know where I want to go first. I read about Merlin in the library this week. He had to be fae. It's so obvious. I want to check out this place called Arthur's Seat, and see if there's anything left over that might give me some good gossip for my paper."

Mia and Luna laughed.

"The papers aren't supposed to be gossip, Vivi," Mia said. "They're supposed to be actual facts."

"Remember, how did the fae and the humans in Scotland interact over the centuries?" Luna asked, lifting her voice into a shrill impression of the teacher's voice.

She didn't sound anything like the teacher, but it made the group laugh. Vivi nodded. "I know that. But it could still be good. Let's get going," Vivi said.

The Unseelie girl's chirpy good mood didn't last long once they reached Scotland. She'd had visions of Arthur's Seat being a palace or a hidden sanctuary of some kind, brimming with ancient knowledge and signs of fae doings she would be able to uncover. Instead, she learned it was a mountain located on an ancient volcano, to which they would have to hike. They stood at the bottom and stared at the mountain.

Carson turned to her after several long, silent moments. "You know, this could actually be a good thing," he said.

"How exactly do you figure that?" Vivi asked.

"Well, we're supposed to be finding all the ways the fae and humans interacted in Scotland. Ancient fae used to hide out near volcanos. The humans worshipped them and their volcanos. We should at least try to see it," Carson said.

"It will be good for you," Luna said, slinging her arm around

Vivi's shoulders. "People say good exercise can clear your mind and help you think better."

"I don't need my mind cleared," Vivi said.

"But it will be a great story," Carson pointed out. "How often do you get a chance to say you climbed a volcano?"

She finally relented, and they headed for the path that led up the mountain. The hike wasn't easy, but halfway up, the challenge became invigorating. Reaching the top of the mountain gave them their reward. At the summit, they could see all the way across the city of Edinburgh. It was stunning, even according to Vivi. They stood there looking out over the city, appreciating the view for a while. Until Vivi stepped back.

"Let's keep exploring," she said.

"What are you looking for?" Carson asked.

"I don't know. But there has to be something. This place wouldn't just be called Arthur's Seat for no reason. There has to be more to it than just a volcano."

They agreed, and roamed around the area, seeing what they could find. After several minutes, they discovered the remains of what looked like an ancient tower.

"Well, there's your castle, Vivi," Mia teased.

"It does look like it was once part of a castle," Vivi agreed. "I wonder what it was."

They went farther and wandered around the base of the crumbling structure. There was nothing to indicate what it was or what significance it had.

"Vivi, can you read the history?" Zander asked. "Is there enough?"

Vivi concentrated on the area for a moment, then nodded. "There's plenty."

Using a similar ability to what she had used with the book from the library, she called up an image of the history of the tower. The first thing they saw was a bunch of teenagers. They danced around the tower and knocked back beers, throwing the bottles into a fire they had built nearby. Some chanted and yelled, while others exchanged sloppy kisses, and tumbled on the ground, drunk.

"That's charming," Mia muttered.

Vivi nodded. "Let me rewind a bit." She rewound the image as far as it would go.

When the image returned, they saw a very old man, hunched over as he put a spell on his home. They couldn't hear what he said or see what he was doing exactly. All they saw was a large bubble forming over it. The dome covered him and his small castle, leaving only the tower where they stood exposed. He wore a blue cloak, held a large walking stick with a gem at the top of it, and had a very long white beard that hung to his waist.

"It's Merlin," Mia said.

The other four looked at her quizzically.

"It could be anybody. We have no idea when this even is," Vivi told her.

"Trust me. I've seen *The Sword in the Stone,* and that is Merlin," she insisted.

They continued to stare at her.

"What?" Carson asked.

"Seriously?" Mia asked, shocked by their seeming lack of knowledge of the movie. "You guys are halflings. There's human in there somewhere. You're telling me you've never seen it?" They just kept staring at her. "I don't have a phone, or I would show you a picture. But trust me. That man is Merlin."

"Okay," Vivi said. "We'll just shelve that one and consider it a possibility. With a whole lot of question marks beside it."

She turned to the image and saw that the man was now looking at her. She admonished herself. He wasn't looking at her. He wasn't really there. This was the history of the area. Whatever was going on in that moment so long ago, he just happened to be looking in the direction she was now standing.

A second later, the man winked at her. Startled by the action so clearly directed at her, Vivi gasped and backed away a few steps. The vision faded, and the other four halflings groaned and shouted their protests.

"Hey!" Carson said. "Where did it go?"

"Bring it back," Zander said. "We didn't even get to see what he was doing."

"I want to know why he was protecting his house," Luna said. "There had to be something interesting going on."

"Bring it back, Vivi," Mia insisted.

Vivi tried to bring the image back, but she couldn't. She was too shaken by the wink to fully concentrate. Instead, she walked around the remains of the castle again, this time in search of signs of the spell shielding the structure. It was possible the spell was still in place, and they might find more of the building.

"Look at this," she said, a while later.

The other four halflings, and the faeries tasked with protecting them, gathered around her.

"What is it?" Zander asked.

Vivi pointed. "Right there. It looks like a cave leading into the volcano."

Curiosity drew them to the mouth of the cave, and into the volcano, almost breathless with anticipation at what they might find when they got inside. None knew what to think when they found nothing but a book.

"It's like the one Vivi found in the library," Mia pointed out.

"Touch it," Vivi said. "See if it reacts to you the way that one did."

Mia marched up to the book and lay her fingertips on the cover. It immediately illuminated, and she pulled her hand away. Vivi and Carson joined her, and each took turns touching the book. It didn't react. Alania and Cinder each tried, followed by the other guardians, Lily and Dalia. None of them changed the book when they touched it. Mia tried again, and again, it glowed brightly.

From the corner of her eye, Vivi spotted something shiny in a far corner of the chamber. She went to it and bent to look. A sudden gust of dust blew up on her, and she sneezed, stumbling backward and landing on her butt. She almost swore, but she bit the words back. "Stupid crickets," she said instead. She got up and brushed herself off. "I'm hungry. Come on. Let's get some lunch."

Mia scooped up the book and put it in her backpack as they left the cave.

"How about afternoon tea at the Holyrood Palace?" Luna suggested.

"That sounds perfect. We are, after all, in the presence of royalty," Vivi teased.

Alania cut her eyes at Vivi, worried about what she might know. She couldn't tell if Vivi was teasing about something she knew was the truth, or if she was just speculating.

CHAPTER THIRTY-THREE

"I don't want the championship to end," Mia said, as they returned to the portal after their day in Edinburgh.

"I knew you would become a big slamball fan," Carson said. "As soon as you started watching, I knew you were going to get hooked."

Mia laughed. "I do like slamball, but that's not what I'm talking about. I'll miss the games, of course, but I'm going to miss exploring Scotland even more. This has been so amazing."

Zander moved closer beside her, and their fingers linked together lightly between them. They exchanged a smile but didn't let it linger too long. The whole day had been filled with ribbing and teasing from the halflings, and even the faeries had joined in. Any time the two of them looked at each other for too long or touched, someone made a comment or a silly sound. It wasn't making her angry, but she'd already had enough for the day.

"We can still go exploring even after the championships are over," Carson pointed out.

"I think she means she's going to miss being able to do it without risking getting in trouble," Luna said. "After the championships are over, I really doubt Elmhurst is going to keep up her blanket permission to go visit Scotland."

"And, no, I'm not going to make portals for us to go whenever we want and pretend it's because we're practicing our Power of Five," Mia said with a laugh.

"Well, you are just going to have to be more specific now, aren't you?" he asked.

They all laughed and went through the portal together. Mia checked the clock on the wall overhead as they all came through. They wanted to make sure they were back for their midnight curfew. Not only did they not want to get in any trouble, but they also didn't want their guardian faeries to be on Elmhurst's bad side for letting them stray from the rules again.

"Perfect," she said with a grin. "Look at that. We're not just on time, we have a whole minute to spare."

"We could have lingered on that walk back to the portal," Vivi said with a roll of her eyes, but nobody missed the smile on her lips.

They took a few steps and noticed dark little figures standing in the shadows. Dan and Steve walked toward them, and held up their left arms, looking at their wrists as if they were checking their watches.

"Guys, you don't wear watches," Carson pointed out. "You're not finding out anything new from staring at your stony little arms. If you want to know what time it is, there's a clock right up on the wall there."

"What are you doing here?" Zander asked.

"Isn't it obvious? They're spying on us for Elmhurst," Vivi snapped.

"We are not!" Dan immediately protested.

"Why would you suggest such a thing?" Steve asked, offended at the accusation.

"Because you've done it ever since we've known you," Luna replied.

"And you're here making sure we're back on time," Mia added.

Both gargoyles opened their mouths as if they were going to try to argue again, but no sound came out. The halflings and the faeries moved around them and headed toward the dorm. They slipped inside and immediately closed the door, locking it.

No one ever came into their room unannounced, except for Elmhurst. But they didn't want to take any chances. Not only would they find the boys in the room, but they'd also catch the five looking at the book they'd been waiting to dig into since finding it in the cave.

Mia eagerly pulled the book from her bag and set it in the middle of the bed. She stared at it for a few seconds before resting her hand on it. It instantly began to glow, and Luna gasped.

"Look," Luna said.

They looked at the first book, which had begun to glow as well. A second later, the book shone brighter, and a scene appeared above it.

"Vivi, are you doing that?" Mia asked.

The Unseelie halfling shook her head. "No. I'm not doing anything."

The book was revealing its secrets without any of them having to call them forward. It was as if the books had been waiting for Mia to put them together. It had to be her. The others knew they weren't the ones who made this happen. Only Mia's touch on the books made them glow. She had initiated something amazing with that touch, and the halflings and faeries fell into a hushed silence to watch.

An image of a beautiful girl appeared in front of them.

"Hello," she said. "I am Princess Caledona."

The girls gasped and exchanged glances.

"The books belonged to the princess," Vivi whispered.

"Which means that couldn't have been Merlin's castle. These books are much older than him," Luna said.

"Unless he was holding one of the books for Caledona," Mia pointed out. "That could explain why he had one. But why would he have anything belonging to her?"

The image of the princess turned and looked directly at Mia. This startled the halfling. She didn't realize such a thing as an interactive vision existed.

"Merlin was a fae mystic who loved humans, especially King Arthur," Princess Caledona explained. "He was also my half-brother."

"Merlin was your brother?" Mia asked, stunned by the revelation.

"Yes. He was born to my father, a fae, and his wife. We don't share a mother," the princess told them.

"Who is your mother?" Carson asked.

"A Pictish woman who caught the attention of my father Callum."

"When was Merlin alive?" Luna asked. "You said he loved King Arthur."

"Merlin died about one hundred years after King Arthur," the princess answered.

"How do you know all this?" Mia asked. "You died well before Merlin was even born."

Princess Caledona smiled. "My spirit lives on between the two books. I am not really gone."

"Why is this all tied to me?" Mia asked. "What do I have to do with any of it? These books respond to me, but I don't understand."

"You are the one who will save the fae from destruction. You must take your rightful place. Along the way, there will be those who will want to kill you. And there will be those who will give their lives for you. You will have many around you who will fiercely protect you from anyone wanting to do you harm. But in the end, it is up to you. You must make the right choices, and you are the only one who can do that. You may have a destiny, but it will only come to fruition if you choose it and follow the right path."

Alania watched, startled by what she saw. She knew they couldn't handle this completely on their own. Without anyone noticing, she slipped out of the room and returned through the portal to the Isle of Skye. She went directly to the pools to get Guardian Myla. Alania knew giving her too many details or trying to explain what was happening without her actually seeing it, would be confusing and take too much time, so she asked the Head Guardian to simply come with her.

Myla followed her, and when she entered the girls' dorm room, she paused. Her eyes fell on the image hovering above the books and tears welled up in them.

"My old friend," she whispered. "I can't believe it's you."

Princess Caledona's eyes filled with tears as she gazed back at the faerie guardian. "I've missed you so much, my dear friend. I'm very happy you've done so well. There are many who want to steal the pools, and you have done an incredible job protecting them. It is very important for you to continue your work. You have a long way to go."

Before anyone could ask any more questions, the image of Princess Caledona disappeared. The halflings protested, demanding that Mia try to bring her back, but Myla held up her hands to quiet them.

"She will not come back until she wants to," Guardian Myla told them. "You must all keep this quiet. Do you understand? It would be best if I take the books with me."

"We found them," Mia pointed out. "And they respond to me. Why should you have them?"

"You may visit the books any time you want, but you have to understand. These books would be extremely dangerous if the wrong fae found them. It would put an even bigger target on Mia, and we can't risk that. If I have the books with me, they are secure and will be guarded with the same power as the pools. No one will be able to get to them and use them for their own purposes. Mia will be safer."

The five looked at each other, silently communicating through their eyes. Finally, they all nodded.

"You can take them," Mia said.

Myla thanked her and took the books into her arms. As the faerie guardian flitted away, Mia thought about Cassia. She wanted to tell her about all this, but she didn't know when she would see her guardian again. This was not something she could say over a phone call.

CHAPTER THIRTY-FOUR

"Something has to be done. It is simply not possible she is so thoroughly enchanted that there is no way to get her DNA," Narco said.

"I'm sorry, Narco. So far, none of the tests we've done have been successful, and my previous attempts have used up all the samples of Mia's blood we had available to us," Orin told him.

"Then we need to get more blood," Narco insisted. "I have to have the proof, although in a way, not being able to get the DNA from her blood is proof in and of itself."

"What do you mean?"

"I already had the strongest suspicion that Mia is the girl I have been looking for. Now that you've proven her hair and her blood are under a spell to prevent anyone from extracting genetic material, I am positive of it. There's no other explanation. Why would a normal halfling need to have those types of protections?"

"That makes sense," Orin told him. "The type of spell needed to veil her DNA this way is extremely hard to do and can be very dangerous. It wouldn't be used for no reason. The only people who would go to the effort and risk of putting on this type of spell are those with very strong motivations for protecting heritage. This isn't just about privacy."

"I want to know more about her," Narco said. "No one seems to know all the details of her life. If I can find out more about her, I can convince my boss of what I already know."

"What do you want to know?"

"I want to know where she comes from and who her parents are on Earth. Is it possible she was staying with foster parents the entire time? Both humans who have no idea who and what she is? Or fae who would be able to protect her as she grew up, and not let the truth of her magic abilities come to the surface when she was young?" Narco suggested. A thought suddenly came to mind. "Or maybe…"

His voice trailed off, and Orin looked at him questioningly. "Or maybe what?"

"We're assuming she was raised by both parents. It's possible she was raised just by her father. And if she was, she could be the child of the woman I killed in Boston seventeen years ago."

"We can find out," Orin said. "Someone can check her school records for any indication of family or friends in the human world. Elmhurst is very strict about records."

"How do you know about what goes on at the academy?" Narco asked.

"I have associates with children at the school. They've told me about how extensive the headmistress is with her record-keeping for each student. Apparently, there have been instances in the past with students disappearing. In some situations, it was magic gone awry, and they were able to find them fairly easily. In others, it wasn't so straightforward. They had to dig through everything they could find about the students, their families, all their associates. Everyone on Earth, and in faerie. Over time, the school made it a requirement to have deeply thorough records, so if anything like that ever happens again, they can more easily search for them," Orin explained.

"So the school will have detailed records of her family and any contacts," Narco said.

Orin nodded. "Yes."

"Then we need to get inside. We need her school records and her computer. You said you know people who have children who go to the academy. Ask if one of them can arrange for you to have a tour."

"A tour?"

"Yes. Pretend you're considering it for a future child or a nephew, or whatever. Come up with something. While Elmhurst is giving you the tour, I will have one of my men go into the office and look through her records."

Three days later, Narco paced through his house while he waited to hear from the man he sent onto the campus behind Orin. It was taking too long. If the records were as thorough as Orin said, Narco should have heard something by now. Finally, a message appeared on his computer. He released a sound of angry exasperation and slammed his hands on the table.

"How could he find nothing?" he shouted.

He couldn't wait any longer. People were on high alert at the campus, watching for him, but it didn't matter. He would have to take the risk.

He created a portal and walked out onto the road leading up to the school. This time, he decided to arrive farther away from campus, in case they had any alarms set up for portals opening near the academy grounds.

Narco put on a different glamour from last time. Since the blasted gargoyles had seen him, he had to create a new persona. This time he used a wig. The Unseelie fae walked across campus as though he belonged there and knew exactly where to go.

Without any issues, other than one halfling looking at him strangely, he went into Mia's dorm room. He could still smell Luna's perfume and knew he had arrived with only seconds to spare. Mia's computer was sitting in the middle of her bed, and he snatched it.

He'd have to give his academy contact a bonus for figuring out a way to get him entry into the dorm after Elmhurst had put a spell on the building barring him. Those halfling fae kids were too easy to bribe. All it took was the promise of getting them into the best college, and they were his to command. The glint in his eyes was evil, and he was almost giddy.

He left the dorm, retraced his steps, and returned through a different portal outside the fence lines. Moments later, he was back at his house, the computer on a table in front of him as he tried to access it. It was protected by far more than just a password. The spell locking it was designed to keep out prying eyes and was far too strong for any halfling to bypass. It took Narco half an hour, but finally, he managed to break through the enchantment and open the laptop.

He sifted through the homework and projects, silly poems and seemingly meaningless lists, everything he thought he'd find in a teenage girl's computer. Finally, he located what he had been looking for. Hidden in a folder filled with pictures was the virtual paper trail of Mia's old life. And in an instant, Narco knew exactly who her father was.

Cassia couldn't ignore the tugging feeling that came with the alert. The small stone, which she had woven into a leather bracelet so it wouldn't stand out to anyone, now glowed a vibrant shade of blue, telling her something was wrong. It had happened before, but each time it had been brief. Now it had been going on for most of the day, and she was getting worried.

Mia's father was missing. The spell she had put on him right after she brought Mia to the academy was meant to trace him in a distant way. It ensured that Cassia would know where he was and if he was following the regular patterns of his life. If he deviated too far, the stone alerted her so she could check in on him. Every other time, it had been something as simple as taking a long weekend, or an assignment at work that took him somewhere he hadn't been before. This time, it wasn't so easy.

Later that day, she sat with Mia, holding her hands as she stared into the young halfling's face. Mia looked shocked, pale, and drawn as she processed what her guardian had told her.

"Are you sure?" she asked.

"Yes," Cassia told her. "I went to check on him, but no one has seen him. He didn't show up for work, and his car is still in the driveway at the house, but he isn't there. He's missing."

Mia jumped up. "We have to go search for him," she said desperately. "We have to find my dad. He's an innocent in all this. He has no clue what's going on, or who I really am."

Cassia shook her head. This was a moment she hadn't prepared for. She had known it would come to this eventually, but she hadn't let herself think about it, not yet. Now, there was no way to avoid it.

"He did know, Mia," she said.

"What?" Mia asked.

"Your father did know who your mother was. Not that she was royalty, but that she was fae, and was in hiding from some very bad people. That was really all he knew. He suspected you were important, but he had no idea how important."

Far away from campus, Narco had just learned the same information. James writhed and gritted his teeth against the pain as the bounty hunter's magic tore through his body without causing any visible injuries. The fae was drawing information from James, forcing his mind and soul to give up the truth because he couldn't trust what the man's tongue might say.

"What's this?" Narco asked, pondering a new piece of information he had just gotten. "You're still hiding secrets."

The interrogation had already revealed that James knew about Mia and had raised her without ever telling her. He had kept her from her heritage and birthright, and also kept everyone searching for her at bay. Now Narco had a new detail that surprised him.

"What?" James asked through gritted teeth, staring defiantly at Narco.

"It seems Mia isn't really a halfling at all. She's not full fae, of course, but to be a halfling, she would have to have one full human parent, and she doesn't."

"What are you talking about?" James asked.

"You don't know?" Narco asked. He used his magic to force out the truth, drawing a growl of pain from the man. "Oh, you didn't. How interesting. I guess I should be the one to tell you that you also have a fae heritage."

"That isn't true," James said.

"You want proof? I can arrange for that."

He called in Orin. When the scientist came in, Narco took a knife and gathered blood from a long slice down James's arm. Orin brought the sample to the table where they had the equipment set up and ran tests. Moments later, he turned to Narco.

"The results are inconclusive," he said.

"What?" Narco snapped.

"I can't get any information from this blood. His DNA must be under the same spell as Mia's. All I can tell you is that he's part-human. That element of his genetic profile is coming up clearly," Orin told him, offering him the sheet of results.

Narco looked at them and gave a mirthless laugh. "It's a shame, really. Your human part shows you are very healthy and would probably have lived a very long life if you had never met Mia's mother. Unfortunately for you, you did. I guess DNA can't predict everything," he said.

"Narco, you have to keep James alive for now," Orin told him.

"Why? He hasn't given me anything valuable."

"We might need him as leverage against Mia," Orin pointed out.

Narco was disappointed. "I was really looking forward to the kill. It's been so long, and I've missed the feeling," he said.

"You will need to learn to control those impulses. They're going to get you in trouble one day," Orin said, shaking his head.

Narco smirked. "No one will ever catch me. I'm far too smart for that."

CHAPTER THIRTY-FIVE

Mia paced the room, her arms crossed over her chest as she tried to cope with the news and the limitations she was under. No one wanted her to go search for her father, and somewhere in her mind, Mia knew it wouldn't help. She would be a liability, at best. At worst, kidnapping her father was only to draw Mia out, and she would fall directly into the trap.

She knew she was too emotional to focus on it, but she was also a complete wreck not doing anything about it either. Mia needed to stay somewhere safe and protected and allow Cassia to do her job.

The door opened, and everyone turned to see Elmhurst on the threshold. She looked somber and reserved as she strode into the room, walking directly to Mia and placing a hand on her shoulder. Her face was a mask of swirling emotions, but she remained tightly controlled.

"Mia, I am so sorry this is happening. You should know that I have some of the best investigators working on it," Elmhurst said, stepping back.

"As do I," Cassia said. "It's Narco. We all know it's Narco. It's just a matter of finding him."

"But what if Narco kills my father before they find him?" Mia asked, tears streaming down her face. Luna stood to comfort her, and Mia leaned into her, though her eyes remained on Cassia.

Cassia cleared her throat. "Frankly, if Narco wanted to kill him, he would have done it already, and made a big show of it," Cassia responded. "He wants to use him for something. Either bait, to get you to reveal yourself where he can catch you, or eventually to use him to trade for you. He might be ruthless, but he's not stupid. Narco will keep your father alive out of a need to use him, and we will catch him before anything else happens. You need to believe that."

"As hard as it may be, Mia, you need to try to continue on as if nothing has happened," Elmhurst added.

Mia looked at Elmhurst as if that was the craziest thing anyone had ever said to her. How could she act like nothing had happened when her father was missing? Elmhurst didn't flinch, though, stoically standing by the door.

"As best you can," said Cassia. "You have to act as normally as you can under the circumstances. Everyone here in this room knows what's going on, and I am sure Elmhurst will alert your teachers to let them know as much as she can about the situation as well."

Elmhurst nodded in confirmation. "I will. We will all wait to see what our contacts can find out, and for Narco to make his next move. It won't be long. As for the rest of you, classes have already begun. I will escort you to your current classes and explain to your instructor what has happened. Mia, you may be excused for the day if you need time to get your emotions under control."

Mia shook her head. "No. I don't want to be alone. I'll go to class."

"Very well," said Elmhurst, looking over her shoulder. "Follow me."

The five students followed her to class. The rest of the day was a blur to Mia, as she floated in and out of being able to focus on her surroundings. At times, she felt disassociated from the school and numb. No anger, no sadness, just an empty well of nothingness.

Then the nothingness would be filled by sadness, or terror, or frustration, or white-hot rage. She was coming out of one of her empty stages when the group shuffled off to their normal practice area. As Vivi put up the protective bubble, Zander collected them to work on the Power of Five.

But as the spell began, Mia's mind drifted away again, and rage filled her heart. She could feel her body shaking with it, and her vision went blurry. Her eyes closed.

"Um, Zander?" asked Carson. "Do you hear—"

The sentence couldn't be finished as the rumble he was drawing attention to turned into an explosion of flame, dirt, and grass. A tree at the side of the bubble was aflame, its branches sparking and shooting orange light high, licking the edge of the protective dome. Vivi closed her eyes as she tried to focus on keeping the shield in place.

"Mia, please, calm down," Zander said, rushing to her.

Another explosion rocked the ground nearby, and everyone but Mia dropped to their bellies. A large oak crashed into the center of what had been their circle. It, too, was ablaze, and Mia's eyes were open, staring deeply into it. The tree went up in flames fast, leaves crackling in the intense heat.

Smoke was filling the bubble, and Vivi was struggling to hold it together. It was risky, though, and she debated dropping it. If she let it down, Mia might start exploding trees where innocent people were. But if Vivi kept the dome in place, they all could all die of smoke inhalation.

Before Vivi made a choice, Elmhurst appeared at the edge of the bubble. She raised her hands, released the protective spell, and Vivi fell over in exhaustion. Striding up to Mia, Elmhurst commanded her attention, and the pressure in the air dissipated.

"All five of you, back to your dorm," she said, her voice rising above her almost-legendary even tone. "Mia, you must learn to control your powers. This is far too dangerous. I know you're worried about your father, but you must get your emotions under control before you hurt someone else…or yourself."

A few days passed, and at the behest of Cassia, the group decided to take a much more controlled Mia to the Slamball World Championship Finals. The Elmhurst Academy had made it into the finals, and the entire school would be there to cheer them on against a halfling academy from France.

After the incident on the practice field, Elmhurst needed a little convincing to let Mia off the campus. Cassia was still working on Elmhurst to reluctantly give permission as they walked the grounds of the school, the gang trailing behind them.

"Seriously, what can happen at a game filled with fae who are specifically on the lookout for something happening in the stands? Mia needs some time to do something other than worry," Cassia argued.

"Fine," Elmhurst said, as they walked past the library. She addressed the group. "You may go to the games, but you must return immediately after."

"I wish I could go," said a voice behind Cassia. She turned to see a dejected Dan on his pedestal.

"It sounds like so much fun," said Steve, pouting.

"I wish you could too," said Mia, her head bowed. "I would feel better if you could."

Dan shifted his weight, and his eyes bulged. "Steve?" he asked beneath his breath.

"Yeah?"

"I just moved my leg," Dan said, sounding confused.

"Hey, I just moved mine," Steve said in surprise.

"No," Elmhurst objected. "Not those two."

Without waiting for permission, Dan and Steve took to the sky, soaring around delightedly in broad daylight. After a few moments of flight, and a heavy sigh from Elmhurst, they returned to the ground beside Mia.

"Thank you, Mia," Steve exclaimed. "Can we go with you now?"

"I hardly see the point in drawing that much attention," Elmhurst said. "You are needed to protect the campus."

"Who's going to mess with a girl who has two gargoyles, though?" Cassia asked, smirking.

Elmhurst sighed heavily again. "Fine," she said. "But when the game is over, you two will return to your normal schedule. Or rather, your *new* normal schedule."

The game was tight, and the score was close. Elmhurst was playing exceptionally well, but the French Cantrell Academy was an even match for them. Mia sat nervously in the stands. With everything going on, the excitement of the game was overwhelming, and she felt like thousands of eyes were watching her and not the game. The blue uniforms of the Cantrell team blurred with the green of the Elmhurst players, and she tried to shake off the tension, and focus on the game.

The third quarter was winding down, and Cantrell had the ball. A quick pass underneath a leaping defender got to an open shooter. He bounced off a trampoline, flipped over the outstretched arms of one of Elmhurst's defenders, and slammed the ball in for the lead. The Cantrell side of the audience went wild, and sudden desperation filled the Elmhurst supporters. Taking the ball on their side of the court, the Elmhurst forwards tried to make a shot, but Cantrell stole the ball and began making their way back down the court.

"You should do something," Zander said, elbowing Mia lightly on the arm.

"Hmm?" Mia responded, having again lost focus.

"We're going to lose," Zander pointed at the court.

Mia gave a short laugh. "I thought you looked down on interference."

"This is the World Championships!" he exclaimed. Mia wondered if that meant when the stakes were high enough that his morality about cheating went out the window.

"No," she responded. "Cheating is cheating. Even in World Championships."

Off in a corner, not too far away, Narco, Orin, and the rest of his team sat in the stands, disguised. They were watching Mia with great interest, but the roar in the stadium was far too loud to hear what they were saying. Narco tried a spell that grew a small weed at their feet to act as a receiver to spy on them, but the crowd was too loud to identify anything other than the occasional word. He swore under his breath and turned to the bogan he had brought as part of his team.

"I need to know what's going on," he muttered. "I need her to get up and leave the stands. When she does, I'll cut her off."

Orin tried to object, to argue that perhaps blowing their cover wasn't the most strategic move, but Mia was standing, and Narco stood with her. He was already walking down the aisle, getting into position to wait for her. Orin shuffled from his seat to join him as they went to a mostly empty stairwell, across from where Mia was standing. She began to leave the stands, with Cinder, Vivi, and Luna joining her. Narco swore again.

"Why does she always have a posse around her?" he spat.

High above him, Dan and Steve were soaring over the stadium, watching the game below. Their attention was fully on the match as they believed Narco couldn't possibly be stupid enough to go after Mia where so many fae were looking for him. They swooped low for a better view of the play on the court, and their shadows passed over Narco, stopping him in his tracks. He looked up and saw something flying overhead.

CHAPTER THIRTY-SIX

Narco watched the dark figures flying overhead and looked away dismissively. Just a bunch of flying monkeys making trouble. His face contorted in distaste, disgusted the league would allow them to attend the games. There should be some sort of screening process, some guidelines creatures had to follow in order to qualify to attend the events. Other, more appropriate beings shouldn't have to be subjected to them.

When he pulled his attention from looking around for an official intending to have the flying monkeys removed, Narco realized that Mia was on the move. Luna, Cinder, and Vivi in tow, she had left her seat, and was headed out of the stands. Narco pulled a folded note from his pocket and pressed it into Orin's palm.

"Take this to Mia, and be sure she reads it," he instructed.

He couldn't take the note up to the halfling himself. The instant he stepped out of the hiding place to approach her, he would be detained. Though he didn't see any security near her, and there wasn't anyone very obviously watching her closely, he knew the measures were there.

Especially now that it was well-known that her father was

missing, Elmhurst would ensure there were plenty of adults on high alert around her. Orin was a different situation. No one knew who he was, nor would anyone have any reason to think he was a threat to Mia in any way. He could walk up to her, hand her the note, and be gone before there was any indication that anything was amiss.

Even if someone did have suspicions, it didn't matter. Narco didn't care if Orin was detained. At this point, his skill set wasn't needed any longer. It wouldn't be much of a loss for Narco if the other man was taken in. As long as Orin kept his mouth shut.

"What do I do if someone asks why I'm giving it to her?" Orin asked.

"Play dumb. Don't give any indication you even know what's inside. When you go up to her, say someone bumped into you in the crowd and asked you to give the note to her. Hand it to her and walk away. Just go somewhere like that's where you were headed in the first place, and like you have no idea that anything else is going on," Narco told him.

Orin nodded and walked toward the halflings.

"Excuse me."

Mia looked away from Vivi to the owner of the deep voice who was standing beside her. A man she didn't recognize held a folded piece of paper out to her.

"Someone in the crowd asked me to give this to you," he said.

She looked at the paper quizzically, then stared back at the man. "Who?"

He shrugged. "Just some guy." He waved it closer, and Mia took it. As soon as the paper left his hand, the man smiled and wandered away, quickly disappearing amongst the other spectators.

"Who was that?" Luna asked.

Mia shook her head. "I don't know. I didn't recognize him."

She didn't think anything of the man, but the paper in her hand intrigued her. She wondered what it could be, and why someone would want it given to her. She opened it. The words written inside the note made her head swim.

"It says I have to meet with Narco, alone, or my father will die. He says to meet him in one hour on the south side of the island," she told the others.

Alania hung back from the three halflings, watching as they moved through the crowd, and saw the strange messenger. He seemed casual and unaffected by the interaction, but his presence bothered her.

She flew higher to watch where he was going. The man strolled through the crowd, and made a few turns and twists, not going to any specific place. Soon, he looped around and walked a wide arc to avoid the halflings, before meeting up with Narco.

As soon as she saw the bounty hunter, Alania shot off toward the stands. Elmhurst and Cassia were sitting there among the others, watching the game. The championship was coming to an end, and despite all they were facing, they had wanted to take some time to experience this together. But they were all on edge, and as soon as Cassia saw the little faerie coming to her, she got to her feet.

"What is it?" she asked.

"Where are the others? Where are Zander and Carson?" Alania asked.

"They went to look for Mia. What's going on?" Elmhurst asked.

"Narco is here," the faerie announced.

Back near the concession stands, Mia felt as though her feet were rooted to the ground. She stared at the note, trying to process the words and decide what she was going to do. She was shaken out of the trance-like state by Cassia's voice.

"Mia, Narco has been spotted. The man who handed you that note is working with him," she announced.

Elmhurst moved slightly away from the group, standing with Mia at her back, and created a shield around them in case Narco was watching. Alania, Lily, Dalia, and Cinder knew he was watching them because *they* were keeping their eyes on him. But the shield would guard them, keeping Mia away from Narco if he did try to come for her.

"What are we going to do?" Cassia asked. "We can't just let him be here and do something like this without stopping him. We've been waiting for him to make himself obvious, and now he has."

"He's not going to go down easily," Elmhurst told her. "It would be too dangerous to go after him now. With this many people around, a confrontation could be disastrous. We need to limit the danger as much as possible."

"I'll go meet him," Mia said.

"What? No. You can't do that," Zander argued.

"Yes, I can. Look, he wants me. That's obvious. He has my father. He's hurt other people. It's all because of me. He's willing to get away from all these other people and not cause any trouble if I'll meet him alone. So, that's what I'll do. I'll go to the south side of the island, and he'll see me there, by myself," she said.

"But she won't be," Cinder added. "She won't be alone. I will be there with the other guardian faeries. We can protect her without Narco knowing we're even there."

"And Dan and Steve will be there as well," Elmhurst offered.

"We will stay in a central spot, and I'll create a pinhole portal," Cassia offered. "My team and I will watch, and as soon as Narco shows up with Mia's father, we will come through."

"Not until you know he's safe," Mia instructed.

Cassia agreed, but the other halflings surged forward.

"You can't do this," Vivi said. "Not alone."

"Mia, it's too dangerous," Luna said. "Even with Cassia and her team watching, something could happen before they even have a chance to get to you."

"Let us go with you. We have been in this together from the beginning. We want to be there and protect you. Remember what Princess Caledona said. You have people who will fiercely protect your safety and not let any harm come to you." Zander reached for her hand.

She held his hand for only a second before letting go, shaking her head as she stepped back from him. "No, Zander. She also said I would have friends along my path that will die for me. I won't let that happen to you. I can't let any of you come with me. You have to stay here," Mia demanded. She turned to Elmhurst. "Headmistress, you have to keep them here."

"I will," Elmhurst said. "It's not an option. None of the rest of you will be allowed to go. I understand your concern and that you believe you could help her. But it is far too dangerous for everyone involved."

"It's already too dangerous for her," Zander pointed out angrily. "This man has been trying to get to her since before she arrived at the academy, and you're just going to serve her up to him on a silver platter."

"If there was a way to get Narco there without Mia, I would do it in a heartbeat. But there isn't. He would see through glamours or spells to create a stand-in for her. He would know if we were trying to deceive him. Mia's father would be killed without question. Mia's own powers, along with the protections of the faeries and gargoyles…this is the best way." Elmhurst's sour face was the only outward indication of her hatred for this plan.

But internally, she was stewing. If there was time to get more trusted fae in place, she would do it. Sadly, this was the only way she could think of to capture Narco and end his pursuit of Mia.

Mia didn't allow herself to feel afraid as she stood in the meeting spot, waiting for Narco. He might be able to sense her fear, and she wasn't going to give him the satisfaction of knowing he affected her in that way. She stood firm, looking around so she would see him coming. It felt like she had been waiting for hours when he finally arrived. But her father wasn't with him. Only the man who had come up to her at the game to hand her the note stood by his side.

Mia took an aggressive step toward him. "Where's my father?" she demanded.

Narco didn't respond immediately. He was scrutinizing their surroundings. He scanned the shadows and hiding places around them. When he was satisfied they were alone, he stepped closer.

Mia kept her eyes locked on him. She wouldn't allow herself to glance up at the faeries he hadn't noticed hiding among the branches of the trees, or the gargoyles flying high enough overhead to not be recognizable.

Narco looked at the man. "All right, „."

Hearing some meaning Mia didn't understand, the man he called Orin turned away. He walked a few feet, opened a portal, and disappeared through it. Moments later, he returned, this time pulling James along with him.

The sight of Mia filled James with even more worry and he lunged toward her, wanting to comfort her. Orin tightened his grip on him, holding him back from going to his daughter.

"Let him go!" Mia shouted angrily. She stared Narco fiercely in the face, refusing to show fear, wanting him to see the threat in her eyes. "Let my father go now. He is human. He has nothing to do with this."

Narco sneered at her and made no move to have James released. "You don't know your father like you think you do," he said.

"What do you mean?" Mia asked through gritted teeth.

"Your father is more than human," Narco sniggered.

"I'm not falling for some stupid trick. Let him go," Mia exclaimed.

"You don't believe me? Why don't you ask him yourself?"

Mia turned to her father, who stared back with wide, sad eyes. But his lips didn't move. Eventually, he looked at his shoes, and Mia's breath hitched. Something more was going on than she knew, but she didn't have time for that now.

"I don't care," she said, at last. She faced Narco. "Let him go. That was the deal."

"New deal," Narco said giddily. "I'll let James go, but only if you go with me without a fuss."

"Mia, no," shouted James, and Orin shook him hard.

"Fine," Mia said, without missing a beat. "But only *after* you let him go. I need to know he is safe before I come with you."

Narco thought about it for a second, rubbing his chin before nodding at Orin. The scientist released James from his grip, and he ran to his daughter, embracing her. Mia embraced him tightly and felt him move his head so he could speak into her ear.

"They are going to double-cross you," he whispered.

"I know," she replied. "I have a plan."

But the portal should have opened by now, and Cassia should have come through. That was the plan. But nothing had happened. Moments ticked by as Mia waited, staring into her father's eyes. Behind him, Narco cleared his throat loudly.

"I really am getting impatient, Mia. We had a deal," he sneered.

"I am saying goodbye to my father," she shouted, hoping to stall for a few more seconds.

"No, you aren't," Narco said, stuffing his hands into his pockets as if he didn't have a care in the world. "You are waiting for your friends to show up. Unfortunately for you, they won't be coming. I saw to it they were distracted."

Mia swallowed hard and winced. So much for that part of the plan. Yet the fear she expected to grip her heart wasn't there. She wasn't afraid, nor was she worried. She was angry.

Exceptionally, extremely angry.

She could feel the anger taking complete control of her, and where she normally stopped it from engulfing her in a flame of hatred, this time she let it pass through, filling her with an energy she had never felt before.

"Mia, what's going on? Why are your hands glowing?" James said, taking a small step away from his daughter. Her eyes rose to his, brimming with tears, and the fire of vengeance beyond them.

"Run," she whispered in a hoarse voice. "Get away."

Before he had a chance to react, her body stiffened, her hands shot out by her sides, and electric sparks flew from her fingertips. A spark struck James, and he fell. The air crackled with sulfur and sparks, and she looked down at him, curled on the ground. He was okay but stunned. It was the only confirmation she needed.

Mia turned to Orin and held out her hand, fingers splayed. Clenching them into a fist, she shot a bolt of electricity that hit the fae in the center of his chest, knocking him several feet back and into unconsciousness. She stepped in front of her father, and faced off with Narco, her eyes narrowed and her jaw set. Mia raised her arm to point at Narco and sent a bolt of electricity at him.

Narco ducked, rolling to the side, and threw up a small blocking shield. The electric bolt bounced off and flew away, and Narco stood there, grinning. He had pulled his hand back, conjuring an attack spell of his own, when a shadow soared over him, low and foreboding. He looked up to see Dan flying at close range, and Steve just behind him. Narco ducked in time to escape the reach of Steve's grasping fingers. From the trees came a warrior band of faeries, and Narco spun to see them. They were coming from every direction.

"What the crickets?" he exclaimed, not knowing which way to turn first.

"Dan, Steve," called Mia. "Take my dad and get him away somewhere safe!"

The gargoyles nodded, and grabbed an arm and a leg, carrying him safely away. Narco was still searching for a way out, and he spotted Orin sprawled on the ground. He elected to save himself. Opening a portal a foot away, he tried to jump through, but he bounced off. The portal closed, and he cast it open again. Before he could move, it was closed once more.

The faeries were now surrounding him, waiting. Outside the protective bubble, Cassia and the gang were shouting to be let in. He was surrounded, with no means of escape. Mia stepped closer and saw her friends, but she didn't drop the shield. She wanted to take care of this on her own.

"Why are you after me?" she shouted, getting his attention. Narco turned to her slowly, an evil, malevolent smile on his face. He laughed.

"I am far from the only one. You can do what you like with me, but there will always be someone after you, Mia. The queens cannot have you left alive. You will suffer death by someone's hands, sooner rather than later."

"Why?" Mia demanded. "Why me? I'm only a halfling, and I am still learning what that even means. There's no way anyone would follow me."

"You are much more than a halfling. And you know it."

Narco rushed at her, firing a ball of energy that missed wildly above her. It was meant to miss, to cause a distraction so he could hit her hard with his fists, but she was ready. Not fooled by the missed shot, Mia side-stepped, sweeping her leg out to kick him in the jaw.

He stumbled away, and charged again, swinging his fists lamely at her. He was no match for her years of Wushu training, and with little difficulty, Mia found an opening and smashed her fist into his face, sending him sprawling backward to land hard on his bottom.

Roaring, he stood again, and Mia shot an electrical ball at him. He ducked out of the way, but she pulled her hand back, casting a spell to bring the bolt curving around like a boomerang. It hit Narco in the back of the head, and then enveloped him. He fell to the ground, motionless, encased in what looked like a small, personal electric storm.

After he stopped twitching and was no longer a danger to anyone, Mia dropped the protective bubble. Cassia and the group rushed in, and they crowded around Narco's body.

CHAPTER THIRTY-EIGHT

Elmhurst couldn't believe what she was seeing as she stood over Narco. The makeshift sarcophagus surrounding him was unlike anything she had ever seen a halfling create. It was truly incredible, and she couldn't help but be impressed at the sight.

"If this were a test, you would have gotten an A-plus, Mia," she said. She looked at the halfling, who still appeared shaken by her experience.

Mia's eyes narrowed slightly. "Um. Thanks," she said.

"No, you don't understand," the headmistress told her. "What you just did is something very rare. I have never seen a halfling accomplish anything even close to it. Most full fae can't even do it. Almost anyone who tried would end up killing the prisoner."

Mia shook her head. "I don't understand. What did I do?" She was confused and slightly disoriented. She didn't even know what had happened or why. Only that as soon as it did, the danger was over.

Cassia smiled at her. "Fan would be so jealous," she commented. Everyone looked at her with confusion, and the smile faded. She stared at each of them in turn. "What? Fan. You know, Fan, the head jailer?" None of them responded, and she shook her head. "Never mind. Anyway, Mia, you created a prison of sorts. When you sent out that blast of electricity, you encapsulated Narco in an inescapable bubble. He won't be able to move, or leave it, for as long as he's trapped within it."

"But he doesn't have anything in there with him. No food or water. He won't be able to survive long," Mia said. "What good is it as a prison?"

"That's the thing. He doesn't need anything else in there with him. The bubble will keep him alive. He can survive in there for up to twenty-three years," Cassia told her.

"Twenty-three years?" Mia asked.

"Give or take, depending on how strong you are," the bounty hunter guardian clarified.

"Then it will probably be closer to fifty years," Zander said.

They all laughed, and Mia looked between Cassia and Elmhurst.

"I still don't think I understand. What does this all mean?" she asked. "What happens to Orin?"

She gestured at the fae still sprawled on the ground. His silver hair clung to his face, and his body looked broken.

Cassia shook her head dismissively. "Don't worry about Orin. I'll take care of him. He won't see the light of day for a very long time. Attacking a halfling at the Slamball World Championships will bring a very long prison sentence, with no chance of a hearing."

"What if he tells people who I am? Narco said he isn't the only one who is after me. He's working for someone else, which means there are other people out there determined to take me out. If they toss him into prison, Orin might start rambling about me to anyone who will listen. If he thinks having information about me could protect him, or get him any sort of better treatment or privileges, he's going to do it. I'll still be in danger."

"I'll see to it he can't say anything about you," Cassia reassured her.

The tone of her voice said she was serious, but Mia still didn't feel secure. "What about Narco? What will happen to him? He's stuck in that bubble for now, but what happens when he gets out? I can't imagine he's going to look at being stuck in an electrical bubble for that long as a time out that has mended his ways and changed his views. He's going to be mad as…crickets," she said.

"Try not to worry about Narco for now," Elmhurst told her. "I will take care of him. You've done everything you needed to. Far more, in fact. We have at least twenty-three years to figure out what to do with him."

Vivi shook her head. "Why should we bother leaving him in the bubble? We should just kill him. He's not going to do anyone any good, and Mia shouldn't have to live the rest of her life afraid because he's still out there."

"I agree," James said. He walked into their circle after the gargoyles released him. "There's no point in keeping him prisoner. He needs to be eliminated. He wasn't just looking for her so he could confirm who she was, and he didn't just have me in order to lure her out. I heard them say as soon as they had Mia, they were going to kill me. Then once they were able to conclusively confirm her identity, they would kill her as well." James put his arm around his daughter's shoulders.

"Killing him now would be too easy," Luna argued. "He has put Mia through so much. Just killing him wouldn't be justice. She deserves to know he's suffering."

"It isn't just that," Carson said. "Like Mia said, Narco was working for somebody, and that means there are other people out there who are a danger to her. Keeping him alive could give us access to information about them. He might not be willing to talk now but give him some time in the bubble, and he could start singing."

The group argued back and forth for several minutes before Elmhurst held up her hands to silence them.

"We have adequate time to consider all of the available options. We don't need to come to a conclusion today. For now, I'll lock him up in the basement of the library where he will be out of the way," she said.

"We'll keep an eye on him," Steve offered.

"Thank you. And now, it's time to go back to the academy. Dan and Steve will need to take their places again," the head-mistress told them. "And I'm sure we all need some rest."

When they returned to the school, the group discovered a dejected campus. Dan and Steve had been drawn back to their pedestals and hadn't had the chance to discover that the Elmhurst Academy Slamball team had lost to the French team by one point.

Mia sighed. "At least we beat Narco." She glanced at her father. "What are you going to do now that you know everything?"

"You should stick close to the school," Elmhurst suggested before he had a chance to answer. "You can learn more, and the time near Mia will do you good."

Alania rushed forward. "Guardian Myla wants James to come to the pools to be trained."

The group looked at her strangely. They didn't understand why Myla would be insistent about something like that. The faerie shared a conspiratorial look with Cinder.

"If James is to survive, he needs to learn how to protect himself," Alania explained. "Who better than guardians to train him?"

Mia felt uncomfortable about the suggestion. This was all so much, happening so fast. She didn't understand what Narco had meant when he had said her father was more than human. She'd never seen any signs he wasn't human, but he had kept her background a secret from her. So maybe he also hid his own from her? *What did any of it mean?*

"I don't know if that's a good idea. I'm afraid for his safety. Wouldn't it be dangerous for him to be around the water of the pools considering how it is supposed to affect humans?" she asked.

Alania waved her hands in the air between them as though brushing away the idea. "That's all a myth. He will be perfectly safe. Besides, your father is not fully human, remember?"

"What does that even mean?" Mia had been wanting to ask about it ever since Narco had mentioned it, but now was the first chance, and she simply couldn't wrap her mind around it all.

Alania stared at James for a few moments, then looked at Mia. "I'm not sure. We should ask Orin about that. But, I can sense something fae about him. It's not much, but there is something inside him." She flittered around his head and sprinkled him with faerie dust.

Instead of floating in the air, she kept him firmly on the ground as she looked inside his aura. What she saw surprised her, but she didn't trust her sight. Alania was going to have to ask the Head Guardian if it was true. Only she would know.

When Alania pulled back, she released the dust that encased James and said, "Yes, he needs to come back with me."

"If that is what will be best for me, I'll do it," James agreed.

"And you will have permission to visit him," Elmhurst assured Mia. "Now that we don't have to hide anything, there's no need for you to be apart like you were. It will be better for both of you if you see each other frequently."

Mia and her father had agreed enthusiastically, relieved to not have to live in separate worlds any longer. Mia was thrilled to have her father back in her life and to be free to share everything with him again. The long months that had stretched between the times they had seen each other had made her feel as though everything wasn't quite real.

Now he would get to know her friends, Zander, and everything she was learning and experiencing because of the fae part of her. She was going to have her dad back in her life again, and she was thrilled.

The only thing missing now was Becky. She adored her friends here, but a part of her still missed her human best friend every day.

James spent the next several days at the academy with Mia, catching up on everything and getting his first taste of a world he never realized was his. Then it was time for Alania, Dalia, and Lily to take him back to Scotland and the faerie pools to begin his training.

Once James left, Mia went to the edge of campus alone. She knew better than to leave the school grounds without permission, but she wanted time to process everything. Her father wasn't human…well, not fully human. What did any of that even mean? She had talked with him about it, but they didn't know. Her father had suggested that he might be able to learn more from the faeries.

She had to discover more about her own powers, just like he had to learn what he was capable of, if anything. Alania had assured them James could be taught to tap into his inner strength. And if nothing else, he would learn how to fight the fae. For surely, this wasn't over with.

After stewing for a few minutes and crying for a few more, Mia wiped the tears from her eyes and turned to find she had company.

"What are you doing here?" She hiccupped and felt her cheeks heat up with embarrassment.

Zander rubbed the back of his neck and smiled wryly. "I thought you might want some company." He shrugged. "And…

um…well, we never did get our date to see the German Vampire team compete."

Mia smirked. "Yeah, turned out those were some of the hardest tickets to get. Who knew, right?" She had known when he had originally asked that they wouldn't be able to get the tickets, but she didn't care. All she had wanted was to spend time with him alone.

Almost from the beginning of the World Championships, they had never been left alone. Even on their one date, they couldn't be alone. But now…

Zander dropped his hand when he realized his palms were wet. He didn't like the idea of spreading sweat all along the back of his neck. Hoping she didn't see it, he wiped his hands along the sides of his slacks.

"I thought maybe we could do something closer to home?" He didn't sound as confident as he normally was, and Zander mentally berated himself. He was the leader of their team, and she liked him, didn't she? So, why was he so dang nervous?

A slow smile spread across Mia's face, and she looked at her feet. "Yes, that would be nice."

Though her answer was more of a whisper, Zander still heard it, and his heart skipped a few beats. "How about dinner in town tomorrow night?"

Mia bit her lip and nodded.

EPILOGUE

The next time James returned to Elmhurst Academy, it was graduation day. He found it hard to believe the day had actually come, and Mia, along with the other halflings, would be graduating from high school. This wasn't the type of graduation he had expected to attend with his daughter when she was young.

Even two years before, he'd had a different vision of what it would be like to watch her graduate from high school and look ahead to what the future held for her. He had believed he would be sitting in the cramped stands around the football field of her high school in Pasadena, looking down at the folding chairs lined up on the grass. The large class of seniors would walk up to a stage built in the same place as for homecoming, pep rallies, and the annual senior picnic.

Instead, he now sat in the luxurious theater of the academy building to watch a group of impressive halfling students accept their diplomas. Of them, a small number stood to be acknowledged with special accolades.

He could barely contain his pride at seeing his daughter standing there among them. She beamed, the traditional fae

247

cloak she wore sparkling with the pins and ribbons she had earned through her studies and exceptional accomplishments.

Though others had been training in their skills and magic throughout their entire lives, she still stood high above them in her capabilities. It had been born into her, a gift from the incredibly powerful princess far back in her bloodline.

For she had to be a descendant of Princess Violet. While he had learned about himself at the faerie pools, he had also learned more about his wife and daughter. Although he didn't know how many generations separated Princess Violet and his wife, Lilliana, one thing was sure—his daughter was a princess.

James knew that power came with risk. It put her in the crosshairs of people who didn't want her to exist. But he didn't want to think about that. Not today. Today was for celebration.

After the graduation ceremony, Elmhurst invited the families to a lavish banquet in the formal hall. Both human and fae came together to eat a decadent feast, enjoy entertainment, and meet each other. The five flitted around together, introducing each other to their families, and then their parents to each other.

Now it was Vivi's turn. She led them up to a stark-looking man James had seen watching Mia throughout the graduation ceremony. Vivi gestured at him. "Father, this is the group I have told you about. This is Luna, Carson, Zander, and Mia. Everyone, this is my father."

He looked less than impressed with them, not bothering to offer an insincere smile. His eyes locked on Mia for a long moment, as though he was contemplating something about her. But he didn't say anything. The group moved on, hurrying to Nicoletta, who stood at a dessert table set to the far side of the room.

"Mom, you don't have to stand with the desserts," Luna told her.

"Principal Elmhurst specifically asked me to make these for the celebration," Nicoletta argued. "She could have had anyone else make desserts. I'm sure the kitchen here at the school is more than capable."

"Not like you," Luna said. "No one can make the decadent creations you do." She scooped up one of the tiny individual cheesecakes her mother had presented on a cut-glass plate and ate it in one bite.

"I just want to make sure everything is all right," Nicoletta said.

"And we want you to enjoy yourself," Luna said.

"She's right. Come on," Carson said, taking Nicoletta's arm and tugging her toward the banquet table. "You deserve this celebration as much as any of us. Without your diner, and all the food you made for us, we wouldn't have made it through. I know I'm going to miss your veggie meatloaf."

Nicoletta laughed and allowed them to take her into the party. The group ate and danced, they sang and enjoyed magical drinks that sparkled and changed colors and flavors as they drank them. The party continued for hours, but finally, the families started drifting away, and soon it was only the Five, Cassia, James, and the faeries that remained. Elmhurst came up to them and gave a satisfied sigh.

"Now that it's just us, I wanted to let you know that Narco is gone," she announced.

Cassia's eyes widened, and she surged to her feet. "Gone? He's gone? He got out of his bubble?" she asked, her voice heavy with worry.

Elmhurst shook her head. "No. All I meant is that I had him moved into a room in the basement and the door concealed with a spell to ensure he's not messed with. Remember, it was Mia who put him in that prison. It will hold him for at least twenty-three years."

"Thank goodness," Cassia said, dropping back in her seat as the others laughed.

"And those years will give us time for Mia to train and learn as much as possible about who she is and what she can do. But that is for another time. For now, the five of you need to focus on college," the headmistress said.

Carson released a celebratory whoop. "I can't wait. I can't believe we all made it into the University of the Northwest."

It was the most prestigious university in the supernatural world, and only the best of the best were accepted there. For most halflings, going to UTN was a dream—something they all aspired to but few considered a possibility.

It would be a tremendous change for the halflings who had never attended anything but fae-based schools. Humans also attended the university and knew nothing of the supernatural programs. The halflings and fae who attended had to be extremely careful not to let the truth about themselves come out. If a human found out about a fae, the human's memory was wiped, and the fae was immediately kicked out of the school.

"What about you, Mia?" Zander asked.

"It will be amazing," she answered, but college wasn't what was on her mind.

"What are you actually thinking about?" Cassia asked.

Mia looked at each of them and released her breath.

"I have twenty-three years to claim my birthright. I'm not going to back down. I know who I am and what I need to do. It's just going to happen about a hundred years sooner than I expected."

Thank you so very much for reading this far, and for finishing up the series! I had such a great time creating this with Michael, and learned a lot! Plus, it was awesome to be able to use my travels in Scotland for the background of this book. In case you didn't know, the faerie pools are real! There may or may not be faeries who guard the entrance to the fae realm living there. You'll have to travel there yourself one day and find out! LOL

I also want to thank the beta readers and editors for doing such a fantastic job with this series! The beta readers read it early on and told us what worked and what didn't work. Then they read it again as we re-wrote scenes. And then they read it again! Some of them read the books 4-5 times before we finally had the finished product. So, a HUGE thank you goes out to them all! Their names are listed in the beginning of the books. 12

And Michael Anderle. I don't know how to thank the man responsible for my career. I wouldn't be an author at all if he hadn't encouraged me or helped me write my first book. Did you know that he even created the cover for my first book? Yup, that's right. He made the very first Eclipse series book. I have changed it up a couple of times since then, and that series is no longer available to purchase, at this time. But, I do plan to re-write it and take the 5 book series and turn it into 3 books and relaunch one day. Maybe I'll include a copy of that first cover so Michael's fans can see how far we've come! LOL

If you have enjoyed this series, you might want to check out other's I've written, like the Miss Claus series. <u>Miss Claus and the Secret Santa</u> is book 1 in a 4-book series about the children of Santa Claus and who Santa really is. Hint: He's not human. You'll find shifters of all sorts throughout this series, so don't miss it! And if you want the prequel for free, you can join my <u>newsletter</u> and get several free books just for signing up! Plus, you'll find out about sales I have throughout the year as well as when I mark books down to FREE on Amazon!

Again, thank you for reading my story. I hope you enjoyed following Mia and her friends around as they learned more about who she really is.

All my best,

Jen

Want more books by J.L. Hendricks?

Check out Miss Claus and Her Secret Santa for a fun and exciting new take on who Santa Claus really is! Did you know he was an Arctic Wolf shifter? You didn't? Then you gotta check out this completed series today!

<u>Miss Claus and Her Secret Santa</u>

ABOUT J.L. HENDRICKS

J.L. Hendricks is a USA Today Bestselling independent author who enjoys many genres, as evidenced by her catalogue of available books. She is currently focused on Clean & Wholesome Romance and Urban Fantasy, but has also written Space Opera, LitRPG, Paranormal, and Christmas books.

This past year has been spent researching the Clean & Wholesome genre for her new pen name, Jenna Hendricks. She also just finished writing an Academy Urban Fantasy series with a very exciting name in the Indie Publishing world.

One thing she learned early on is to accept help from others in the Indie world, and she is very grateful to those who have helped her along the way! The Indie publishing world is full of extremely nice and helpful authors, which is what makes this the best job she's ever had.

In early 2016 she decided to finally write, and finish a book, because of a few friends who encouraged her to do so. She hopes her stories entertain you and can bring a laugh on occasion.

Actually, it was her roommate's cat who talked her into staying at home to be her minion all day long! Pyper truly believes that J.L. is here to serve her alone.

Come and chat with J.L. on Facebook at:
https://www.facebook.com/JLHendricksAuthor/

And check out her Amazon author page at:
http://jlhendricksauthor.com/62fp

But don't forget her website and blog at:
https://jlhendricksauthor.com/

The Voodoo Dolls

Book 0: Magic's Not Real
Book 1: New Orleans Magic
Book 2: Hurricane of Magic
Book 3: Council of Magic

Worlds Away Series
Book 0: Worlds Revealed (join my Newsletter to get this exclusive freebie)
Book 1: Worlds Away
Book 2: Worlds Collide
Book 2.5: Worlds Explode
Book 3: Worlds Entwined

A Shifter Christmas Romance Series
Book 0: Santa Meets Mrs. Claus
Book 1: Miss Claus and the Secret Santa
Book 2: Miss Claus under the Mistletoe
Book 3: Miss Claus and the Christmas Wedding

Book 4: Miss Claus and Her Polar Opposite

The FBI Dragon Chronicles
Book 1: A Ritual of Fire
Book 2: A Ritual of Death
Book 3: A Ritual of Conquest

Chronicles Of The Unwanted Princess
(with Michael Anderle)
Book 1: The Portal of Chance
Book 2: The Forbidden Portal
Book 3: The Emerald Portal

See these titles and more at https://www.jlhendricksauthor.com/

CONNECT WITH THE AUTHORS

Connect with J.L. Hendricks

Facebook:
https://www.facebook.com/JLHendricksAuthor/

Amazon:
http://jlhendricksauthor.com/62fp

Website:
https://jlhendricksauthor.com/

Connect with Michael Anderle

Website: http://lmbpn.com

Email List: http://lmbpn.com/email/

Social Media:

https://www.facebook.com/LMBPNPublishing

https://twitter.com/lmbpn

https://www.instagram.com/lmbpn_publishing/

https://www.bookbub.com/authors/michael-anderle